HAVE A NYC 3
New York Short Stories

Peter Carlaftes & Kat Georges

EDITORS

THREE ROOMS PRESS
New York, NY

Have a NYC 3

First Edition

ISBN 978-0-9895125-2-7
ISSN 2333-1291 (print)

Editors: Peter Carlaftes & Kat Georges

Cover and Interior Design:
KG Design International
katgeorges.com

Published by
Three Rooms Press, New York, NY
threeroomspress.com

To the memory of
Philip Seymour Hoffman

INTRODUCTION

Think you are ready to take on these streets?

New York City breathes life into millions of people. Sends them off at different times of day and night to jobs and hopes and crimes and heart.

The City takes your breath away. Sometimes forever.

But its memory is short. That's your only edge. To take it on with all your might. Dreams die hard or they never get born.

Nothing lasts as long as the City itself, and its tales which begin on the streets.

CONTENTS

OUT WITH THE TRASH

BY KAT GEORGES

"I don't care what you say—I'm not going!" Andrew hissed. He'd said the same thing for the past three weeks, ever since news came about the move.

The other garden gnomes—nineteen of them—stopped paying attention to him days ago. And now, with moving day finally here, most of them were smiling with anticipation, thrilled at the idea of relocating.

When you're a gnome, it doesn't happen often.

Some of the gnomes had been on this West Village rooftop more than twelve years—part of a growing collection of Jemi and Aaron, the apartment's tenants. Jemi—short for Jemina—was a part-time musician who bragged to friends at her summer barbecues that the gnomes were a source of inspiration. Otherwise, she ignored them. Aaron had a real passion for gnomes. He had built this collection carefully over the years and arranged the gnomes in a semi-circle on a rectangular raised area of the black tar-covered roof, facing toward the back sliding glass door of the apartment, facing away from a carefully tended garden of assorted potted plants.

Most were "authentic" gnomes, crafted in the Austrian-Germanic style: just over a foot tall, sporting tall pointy hats over bearded faces, belted tunics, and short baggy trousers tucked into tiny boots. A few were Disney aberrations: barbarized clones of the commercial version of Snow White's seven dwarves, or cute knockoffs sporting Yankees logos. Errant gifts from well-meaning friends.

Without Aaron, all of the gnomes would have been thrown out years ago. Jemi tolerated gnomes the way vegans tolerate vegetarians. She put up with them. But since she started packing, she secretly wanted them gone.

The news about the move first came to light when the gnomes overheard Jemi making a few phone calls three weeks ago, while she lounged on an outdoor chair on an unseasonably warm January weekend. A few days later, Aaron confirmed, shouting to Jemi from the roof that they would just leave most of the potted plants.

"And the gnomes, too," Jemi yelled back. "Get rid of them, right?"

"No," Aaron shouted, his voice uncharacteristically firm and commanding. "We're definitely bringing our gnomes."

Soon, rumors about the new pad ran rampant as details were picked up here and there in overheard snippets of conversation. It was in Washington Heights; it had a great view of the George Washington bridge; it was much larger and—best of all—it came with a beautiful, giant outdoor terrace. A perfect new home.

Most of the gnomes were excited about going. Today, at sunrise, they toasted each other with dew. To travelling! To adventure! To getting the hell out of the West Village—It lost its soul years ago.

"Now, it used to be the best part of New York," reminisced Douglas, a gentle-looking bearded gnome with a faded blue coat and pale teal pointed hat. "I should know—I've been here longer than any of you." Which was almost true.

Douglas was one of three gnomes—Andrew among them—who had been at the Bleecker Street apartment from the beginning.

"I remember back in the Sixties," Douglas continued, "when Dylan was just starting out—"

"Bullshit!" screamed Andrew. "Stop saying you were here in the Sixties. You weren't even born then."

"Well, shortly thereafter . . ."

"Geez!" Happy exclaimed. "There they go again— same argument since the day I arrived."

"Shut up, you Disney faker," Andrew shouted, "I'll knock you over and bust you into a thousand pebbles."

Berndt sighed, "Guys, *Beruhigen Sie sich!* Calm down! Moving is *stressig* enough without petty name-calling and *die Worte des Ängers*." An even-tempered authentic Austrian gnome carefully selected by Aaron on a long-ago trip to Graz, Berndt kept his hands forever locked behind his back, revealing a pale green belted tunic over dark baggy pants tucked into his worn boots. His bearded face revealed wizened eyes under a pointed red cone hat.

Douglas agreed. "There's really nothing we can do so let's just stay cool and go with the flow."

"Go with the flow?" Andrew laughed. "Don't tell me to go with the flow. Someone has to take a stand."

"You've got no choice," Douglas said. "You're just a gnome."

"I'm not going," Andrew said. And this time, no one argued.

For a week, boxes had been piling up inside the apartment. The gnomes watched from the rooftop as dishes were carefully wrapped in newspaper, clothes stuffed into large plastic bags, furniture turned on end, bookshelves dismantled.

The books. Andrew noticed a few days ago. The other gnomes must have seen, but pretended nothing was wrong. Typical. The books were not being carefully packed into boxes. They were being thrown into bags, carelessly. Pages tore. Bindings broke. He could hear Jemi occasionally exclaim, "I'm so glad to be lightening up!"

"Lightening up" meant getting rid of things. Treating books like trash. Throwing them away. And it wasn't just a few outdated self-help books. Jemi threw out almost all of the books that she and Aaron had collected over the years. "These are so heavy! Thank god we don't have to move them!"

For hours, Andrew watched Jemi maniacally shove book after book into heavy green plastic trash bags, which she later instructed Aaron to take out to the sidewalk with the rest of the garbage. "I've got the ones I want on Kindle," she stated coldly, when Aaron started to pull a few out of the bags. "In a month or so, we'll forget we even had them. Starting clean. It's all good."

Andrew thought hard. The books were so easy to get rid of. What about him and the other gnomes? Aaron had said he was taking them all to the new pad, but Jemi was the real ruler of this household. One flip of her henna-dyed hair and a stern look and Aaron complied with her every demand. Andrew knew, that if the gnomes made it all the way to the new apartment, chances were that Jemi would decide that they just didn't fit in.

Andrew suddenly felt tired and old. He glanced over at the other gnomes. Berndt with his wise face; Douglas with the blue hat and droopy eyes; the three Disney faux gnome copies who didn't really belong— Happy, Dopey and Doc—yeah, sure—get rid of *them*. Then again—no. Even the faux gnomes deserved continued existence. If one was tossed, they all would be, sooner or later.

Before long, the packing of the gnomes began. Aaron came out with a pile of newspapers and two large moving boxes. Jemi carried out some more newspaper and sat it down next to Aaron. "I'm going to miss this roof, this garden," she sighed.

"Well, at least you won't have to miss these little guys," Aaron smiled, nodding toward Andrew and the others. Jemi scowled. "Let's get them packed up nice so we don't break anyone," Aaron whispered.

On cue, Jemi's smart phone buzzed and she hopped up and rushed into the apartment. "Be right back," she swore.

"Yeah, right," Andrew scoffed.

Aaron started at the far end. He gently picked up Berndt, laid him on a few sheets of spread out newspaper, rolled him in it, and sealed the ends with tape. Then he carefully placed Berndt in the box.

Andrew heard Berndt's muffled gnome farewell, "*Auf Wiedersehen, meinen Herren!* See you uptown!"

Andrew shouted, "Not me! I'm not going!"

The faux gnomes giggled, "Yes, you are! Yes, you are!"

Aaron began wrapping the next gnome, a faded orange fellow from Berlin.

One by one, each gnome was packed. When Aaron was halfway through, Jemi came back and looked at the remaining gnomes distastefully. "Do we really have to take them all?" she asked. "They're dirty and old. We don't really need to cart them all with us—right?"

On any other subject, Aaron would have reluctantly agreed. But the gnomes were his.

"Sorry," he said flatly. "Can't leave them here—collector's items."

Andrew sniffed. "Collector's item, indeed. Is that what you call something that's been around for awhile? Yo, Aaron—maybe you should call your old lady a collector's item—*right?*"

"Cool it, Andrew," Douglas snapped. "I'm stressed out enough. Chill out."

"He can't hear me. And I'm not going," Andrew snapped.

Douglas sighed. "I heard you the first thousand times. Pipe down."

Aaron stood and stretched, and asked Jemi, "Babe, can you help me tape up the first box?"

"Sure, babe."

"Wanna get these in the moving van first so they don't get damaged," Aaron said. "They say that first in is the best place for your breakables."

"I'll put the dishes there too, then" Jemi said.

Andrew smirked. "Such brilliant conversationalists! Enjoy them uptown, with your freakin' view of the GW Bridge! Makes me crumble, just thinking about it."

Aaron and Jemi carried the gnome-filled box inside the apartment.

"Like it or not—you're coming, too," Douglas insisted.

Aaron came back and with a heavy sigh, sat down, and began wrapping again. Ten gnomes left. Eight. Five. Now only Andrew and Douglas remained.

"Not going. Not going," Andrew chanted.

Aaron grabbed Douglas, who shouted, "See you on the other end of the city!" before he was rolled in the newspaper and placed in the box.

"Jemi!" Aaron shouted. "Help me tape this box."

All the other gnomes were gone, and there was no more room in the box for him. Maybe . . . maybe . . . maybe his wish would come true.

Jemi pranced out of the apartment and knelt near the box. "Aw, look," she said, sarcastically. "One of them didn't fit."

"We'll carry it in the cab," Aaron said, running the tape across the box top.

"Geez, Aaron!" Jemi whined. "Don't you have enough? I mean—can't we just forget about *one* of them? Grow up!" She stomped back into the apartment.

Aaron followed her inside with the second box of gnomes. Andrew heard muffled yelling. A door slammed. Someone stomped down the stairs. Then—silence. A few minutes later, Aaron came back outside, eyes a bit glazed. *Stoner*, Andrew sniffed.

Aaron lifted Andrew gently. "Well, old buddy—" he sniffed. "Guess the ol' lady gets her way—this time."

Try—every time, Andrew thought.

Aaron carried Andrew to the furthest corner of the rooftop and sat him down. "Here you go, buddy. Best view in the place," Aaron said. "Maybe they'll just let you stay here forever." He turned quickly, and stumbled back into the apartment. By sunset, he and Jemi and everything they owned were gone.

"Wow!" Andrew sang, glancing around. "I did it! I'm really not going! *Whoo-hoo!* . . . "

For two days, Andrew had the roof to himself. "This is living!" he exclaimed. "I hate roommates! Never again! Never again . . ."

Just after dawn on the third day, a crew of six young dark-skinned workers arrived. Andrew watched as they shoved the remaining potted plants into trash cans and carted them off the roof. In the apartment, they threw away a few remaining items: old ice cube trays, a poster of some Irish band, two boxes of books that never made it to the curb. They vacuumed inside and swept outside. They emptied the refrigerator, polished countertops, scrubbed the stove, cleaned the oven, replaced light bulbs, dusted walls, washed windows. After a few hours, they sat down on the little wall surrounding the rooftop, sipped coffee and relaxed.

An older man, with thinning white hair, dressed in a tailored blue suit showed up in the apartment and began inspecting their work. He opened cabinets and drawers, ran a finger across the stove top and sniffed it, made sure the windows were clean. Then he sauntered onto the rooftop. The six workers stood up.

"That's all right . . . Sit down, boys—go on," the older man said. "*Siéntense, por favor.*"

They sat down, keeping their eyes on him.

The man examined the rooftop carefully, thoroughly, without moving far from the entrance to the apartment. He was just about to turn away when something caught his eye.

"What's that?" he asked, pointing. "That—over there."

Andrew knew he had been spotted. The leader of the work crew got up and walked quickly over to him, as another explained to the man that they were sorry for not seeing it earlier. The worker grabbed Andrew and rushed him back over to the man.

"*No sé lo que es,*" the crew chief spewed. "*Lo siento, es basura.*"

"Wait."

The old man lifted Andrew out of the worker's hands.

"A gnome?" he asked, to no one in particular. "What the hell is a gnome doing in Manhattan?"

He tucked Andrew under his arm and reached into his pocket, extracted an envelope and gave it to the crew chief. "Here's your pay—nice work boys. You can go. Call you again soon. *Adios.*"

The workers left, and the man held Andrew up and examined him closely: his faded red cone cap topping his weathered, bearded face; the belted yellow jacket over faded black pants tucked into worn boots. The man seemed to be remembering something from long ago.

Andrew glanced at his face and knew: The man was remembering that the West Village used to be filled with oddities just like him: handmade sculptures, handmade people, people who didn't mind having rooftop gardens filled with gnomes. Music in the air, ideas flowing in coffee houses, creation, plans, dreams. Rent that people could afford, without roommates. Stores that sold handmade jewelry, fruit, knickknacks. No chain stores! No frozen yogurt stands! No artisanal pizza! No gastro pubs! No foodies! Andrew gazed at the man, hopeful at last.

The man tucked Andrew under his arm and strode back into the apartment, locking the sliding door behind him.

"Well, little fellow—time to go. No place for you here anymore."

"What?!" Andrew screamed. "Wait, buddy! I belong here! Let me go!"

The man left Andrew on the curb with the other trash.

A few days later, far uptown, Aaron wore a mischievous smile. Jemi finally noticed. "What are you so happy about?" she pried. "Is the cable guy coming over today—or what?"

"Nope. Better." He spilled. "Remember that gnome? The one you made me leave downtown?"

"I should have made you leave all of them."

"Look!" He proudly held his iPad toward her. "Found this on Facebook."

Jemi grabbed the iPad, swiped a few times, then handed it back. "Don't get it."

"It's him. That gnome? The one we left? He has his own Facebook page!" Aaron beamed. "Apparently the landlord threw him out with the trash, but someone down there must've found him and now he's like some kind of mascot—taking photos—he calls them selfies, haha!—at all kinds of cool places downtown!"

"Cute," Jemi sighed.

"Don't you see? He's still happening, he's around. And he looks happy! He's got 10,000 followers already."

"That's more than me." Jemi said flatly. "Total bullshit. Damn . . . "

Out on the large terrace, nineteen gnomes giggled.

"Did you hear that?" Douglas beamed. "Our pal Andrew! He's famous! I knew he'd make it! Here's to Andrew—the greatest of us all! A new legend is born!"

The gnomes cheered in unison. Then, together, they stared back toward the George Washington Bridge, and enjoyed the final moments of a gorgeous sunset.

MEMORY THE NEXT

BY BONNY FINBERG

He'd been forgetting where he put things—if they were merely misplaced or lost for good. Today was especially bad. He'd paid for his lunch and left the table carrying the empty water glass. He hadn't discovered it until he was at the door of the restaurant. He'd joked with the cashier as he handed it to her, saying something about the drawbacks of cutting out coffee. She'd laughed politely and said not to worry.

Frankly, he was worried. The truth was, it could be the early stages of dementia. The senior moment jokes were wearing thin as his hair, and he spent more time looking for things than doing the things he used to. He couldn't remember the last time he'd been naked in bed with a woman.

He was habitually distracted, submitting to anything and everything. Every new building that replaced an old one sent him into a quiet rage. They seemed to be sprouting up everywhere, stiff beehives making their way downtown along the main avenue near his apartment. Small tenements and creaky loft buildings sat in borrowed time. Jackhammers and dust had become part of the atmosphere in the way the ice cream man's tinkling bell had been, the old man in a worn suit singing 'Ohhhld clohhthes...Ohhhhld clohhhhthes' in the courtyard under his bedroom window. The man with the number tattooed on his arm who would stand in the courtyard at dusk and play the violin. People would throw down change in brown paper bags. This was before he understood that these were not ordinary things.

Now, there was no courtyard. Beautiful People passed him in the street, phone in one hand, coffee in the other, water bottles conveniently hung from net tubes attached to their backpacks. They worked in the beehives so they could afford to live, eat, and talk on the phone in whatever reprocessed authenticity was left. He tried to avoid Little L.A. where Europeans came to spend their strong currency on more than his measly pensioner's dollar could buy.

In winter, he hardly went outside. Now the weather was turning warm and war was everywhere. He walked to the park, past stores selling things he didn't need or want, but might make life more interesting or comfortable, past apartments which, at one time, no one with money or status would dream of inhabiting, but now they paid good money to walk up six flights to a renovated box with cheap new appliances, eat micro-waved leftovers from last night's take-out in front of their large flat-screened TVs, and watch mediocre independent films, all for a price that at one time could have bought an eleven room house in a privileged suburb.

A couple walked by. He overheard the woman say, "I'm one of those people who has deep feelings." The man looked at her and said, "That's okay. I like people who have deep feelings."

How long had it been since he'd been naked in bed with a woman? Lola Schwartzberg. She never touched a drop. A freight train could have been coming toward her and she would have stared it down. She went barefoot, even at dinner parties, and rolled up her pants like she was planning to walk in a river. Everything she did, she did without apology. She was so comfortable in her skin that whatever she did was okay, in fact charming, to everyone. Except him. What he'd found charming in the beginning ultimately sparked his irritation. She had no use for it and told him he was uptight, jealous, and a prick. So that was the end of that. He heard she went off to Costa Rica with her Brazilian doorman slash aspiring novelist.

Why did he sometimes feel like he might hurt someone? His days seemed to consist of listening to snippets of conversation overheard on the frenzied streets and looking for lost things or avoiding looking for lost things inside the confusion of his apartment. A whole day could go by when he spoke to no one. He hated going out where everyone was busy with devices to keep them from forgetting what they had to know, all of which seemed pointless. Memory had become something that could be bought, stored, and retrieved at will. He had no access to these devices. It was necessary to write things down on little scraps of paper and stick them to various spots on the wall, or the refrigerator. After a while the slips of paper blended into the rest of the clutter and became part of the general blur of things.

Sometimes he thought he'd be better off if he moved into the bathroom where there was less disorder. Bring in a hot plate, put a mattress in the bathtub and plug in a radio and TV. He'd have to run a phone line. These thoughts made him feel crazy. He needed more sleep. He slept too much. He was impatient for things to happen. He couldn't keep pace. He was bored and lonely. There were too many people making demands.

Someone was cooking. He smelled potatoes and roasting meat. A television flickered in one of the banks of windows across the street. He turned on the radio. He threw some sliced onion into a pan of melting butter, then some eggs. He thought about how certain things were so automatic you didn't have to remember to do them, or how to do them. Or not. This made him feel a little reassured. He took a plate and utensils from the dish drainer and pushed some things aside to make a clear space on the table. He picked up the magazine article he'd started at breakfast and began to read. He imagined someone knocking at his door. The Chinese girl down the hall who designed logos for corporations. He imagined her asking him for salt or milk. No one did that anymore, no one knew anyone well enough to ask for what amounted to a handout. People bought and sold, came and went. They barely looked at each other getting on and off the elevator. He imagined the Chinese girl naked in his bed, it didn't matter how she got there, the next morning sitting at his table, which she'd cleaned and set with matching plates, serving French toast with bacon from a platter he'd forgotten he owned.

He went back to his magazine. Mingus sang on the radio, something about eating chicken potpie. He wanted to call someone. He looked through his phone book. Every name recalled some personality flaw, some problem that he didn't want to listen to or be reminded of. He turned on the TV and checked the channels. No one finished a sentence before he flipped to the next—one after another. He turned if off and took out a record at random, a Tunisian singer. He sat on the couch and let his eyes follow the line of the curtains. They fell in a soft V of white lace, lit by a low sun. He watched the light change until there was no more. The record had stopped hours ago.

LUSTRUM AT THE FLUSHING RKO

BY KIRPAL GORDON

Although seventh grader Colleen Greenleaf had done her research, she knew she was losing the argument.

"You said to choose a name that holds special meaning."

"No one has ever taken X for a Confirmation name."

"I've looked up a lot of names. X says so much to me."

"The bishop's performing the sacrament. I can't allow it!"

"Why?"

"It's simply not Catholic, Colleen."

"But I'm Catholic and would be more so as Colleen X."

It was May 1966. Earlier that week, Colleen had received an F on "X: How Malcolm Little Became Malik Shabazz," a book report on his recently published autobiography, and now she realized the failing grade, her first ever, was a miscalculation on her part. She'd compared the fast lives of Malcolm and Saint Augustine, how their confessions spoke to her of the power of redemption. She'd also remarked on the black pride side of Malcolm's ministry, how converts to Roman Catholicism like the Irish, thanks to eight hundred years of the English, faced a similar journey out of assumed inferiority and indentured servitude. What better proof of being right than a failing grade she thought. She wanted the name, Colleen X, to remind her of Ireland's Celtic twilight amidst the Vatican's pinkie ring pageantry.

"Forget X," her mother said.

"Take the name of a saint," Sister Peter John said.

"You're a saint, Sister. Peter John, then."

"Those are male names, Colleen."

"Then your name, Mom."

"Not my name."

"Because Oona's the goddess of witches and fairies?"

"Pick a name right now, young lady, or I'll pick one for you. I'll not have you wasting the good sister's time."

"Joan of Arc then. If I can't have your names, and you two mean the most to me, I ought to have a warrior's name since I'm getting enrolled in the army of Christ," she said, hoping to sound old enough to make her own decisions.

To re-acquaint her with her actual status, the nun told her to wait outside in the hall with her face to the wall while the adults discussed her fate. Colleen gave the wall a few minutes but soon walked over to the window and looked out. Beyond the muddy parking lot the convent grass was singing. Purple and crimson rhododendrons bloomed around Our Lady's grotto where nuns were arranging lilies. All week long during the May Pole dances and song rehearsals for Mary, Queen of May, she sensed that this celebration had older roots. She'd researched the subject at the Whitestone library and found it to be so.

Dismissed by the nun, she raced down the stairs and got in the family car though she did not share what she'd learned of May Day with her mom. In the cold silences and mean looks on the ride home, she got the distinct impression that sassing the nuns or making fun of the Church were not suitable pursuits for a young lady such as herself. At dinner she discovered seen-and-not-heard to be the better part of valor.

However, the next morning she awoke and the bed was bloody. Frightened, she ran to the kitchen, showed her mother and insisted she was too distraught to go to school. Her mom handed her a sanitary napkin, alluded to her predicament as the curse and insisted she not miss the school bus or there would be hell to pay.

Intrigued by her new status as a childbearing maiden, she sat on the school bus reflecting on how silent her mother had become in the face of her first period. She knew this wasn't personal, that her mom probably grew up thinking sex was something shameful and forbidden, not a proper topic of conversation, whereas she thought sex full of innuendo and allure leading to something fun and joyous. Thinking back to the nun's lecture on abstinence, virginity, and self-control versus disgraceful coitus, criminal abortion, and unwanted babies, she decided the church authorities didn't know much about sex. That's why an eighty-year-old pastor counseled young newlyweds, why a drunken priest drove the altar boys home in the parish car, and why many Irish couples, convinced that birth control was a sin, had more kids than they could feed. Reflecting on Malcolm's message of self-determination, she decided X would remain her Confirmation name no matter what pretense she would have to play out for the folks and the officials.

Getting off the big yellow bus, Colleen X walked up the fifty-four steps to All Sorrows Grammar School and took her seat in class as the nun finished the drawing. A disk of white chalk, a sun in a sky of blackboard: That was one's soul. It was the final lesson before Confirmation, and she suspected a soul that white was more like a Sunday dress about to get soiled or spoiled by her tomboy antics. Unlike her dress, her blackened soul required confession, contrition and communion to grow the white back. She wondered if the nun had fallen captive to her own metaphor: the soul had no color or form. It wasn't a thing but an indwelling within consciousness. Since it was invisible, immortal and immutable, it couldn't get soiled or spoiled by anything material she did or did not do. No, she realized, this fallacy in confusing spiritual with material was driven by fear and concocted by the Holy Roman Empire to keep her obedient and pure.

If there were two paths to knowledge—sharing the curiosity and getting your knees dirty or remaining pure and obedient—Colleen X found a higher calling in curiosity. She understood that mortality and sexual knowledge were the real crimes out of Genesis that expelled Adam and Eve from Eden and made childbirth work and pain. But it was also a mysterious life. It was not the inheritance of an invented original sin but a real dance band playing soul music. To move her whole body rhythmically with a handsome young man like Hector Correo in the motion that replicated the motion that had conceived her was the climb up out of the solitude of adolescence into the duet of adulthood. She wanted to dance the Watusi and whatever it was that James Brown did.

So when *The Tablet*, a weekly tabloid of worldwide Church activity, arrived, and the nun suggested the class read the good news of the missionaries fighting godless Communism in the Soviet Union, Colleen X turned instead to the movie listings from the Legion of Decency, a committee of upstanding laity who recommended by category—and delivered with the gravitas of a papal encyclical—what films released from Hollywood Babylon that Catholic school children needed to be protected from. She noticed that a new release, *Pagan Spring, B.C.,* was now on the top of the XXX list, the most objectionable.

The next morning she checked the *Daily News* and discovered the film was playing at the RKO Keith's in Flushing. Had she not been grounded for wanting to be confirmed X, she would have pleaded with her mom to let her go on the bus to the Saturday matinee by herself, but being punished for doing nothing wrong necessitated a declaration of independence. While her mom shopped for groceries and her dad worked in the basement and her older brothers played ball in the park, Colleen X picked up the phone, dialed and waited for a response.

"Hello?"

"Hector?"

"Yeah. Colleen?"

"Yeah. I'm going to the RKO. Wanna meet me there?"

"Yeah. When are you leaving?"

"Now. The movie starts in thirty minutes."

"Okay, I'll meet you inside."

Colleen X hung up the phone, slipped out of the house, and walked to the bus stop. Warned by her mom that the neighborhood was getting bad with dope peddlers known to frequent the pizzeria in order to put dope in the dough, she stood in front of the pizza parlor but saw no one who looked suspicious. When she got on the Q-15 headed for Main Street, rather than worrying about her descent into a widening snake pit of sin, Colleen X felt she was taking her life into her own hands.

She also knew that without an accompanying adult she couldn't get into the picture, so she had padded her new training bra and had spent a lot of time tarting herself up with her mother's cosmetics in order to look older. Luckily, she convinced the ticket lady to sell her an adult admission. Although this eliminated any popcorn, candy, or bus fare home, she didn't care. She walked through two sets of doors and stood in the center of the immense lobby of the RKO Keith's movie palace next to a three-tiered water fountain and felt the hot afternoon slip into cool eternity. The sound the water made throughout the lobby was reassuring, and her eyes adjusted to the hushed, indirect lighting which cast the walls of the balcony in sensual golden shadows. Unlike the interior of the church of Our Lady of All Sorrows which caught heavenly rays of sun illuminating stained glass windows, the round lobby was bathed in a permanent twilight, what the nuns called the witching hour, a sky whose soft blues darkened to deep purples as they reached higher amidst floating clouds and glittering stars.

Studying the decorative trim on the sweeping staircase, the ornate balustrades, the thick red carpet, the Spanish colonial parapets, she marveled at the elaborately sculptured Moorish revival columns that resembled entwining serpents reaching upward from under the earth. She felt rivers open up inside her where caves led to secret ceremonies.

Domed ceiling of my star-crossed twilight, she prayed, I am this labyrinth; I am the anatomy that makes Jesus incarnate. Mother of God, it's the fate of Lucifer bearing light I accept; Heaven's only a projection booth, a room in my head no one can enter, and I long to break open in shared loving desire. If this be hubris, if loss and abandonment, shame and misery are all I'll know, I'll suffer the pagan price, just like my ancestors, only let me square up later for right now I want to stand and be counted in this lustrum at the RKO among other initiates curious and intrepid.

"Colleen?"

She turned and there stood a smiling Hector Correo.

"You look older," he said admiringly.

The lights flashed off and on so they walked up the stairs, entered the balcony and sat in the dark.

Pagan Spring, B.C. proved to be as boring as *The Tablet,* unable to live up to its billing as a revealer of ancient mysteries, but Hector knew how to kiss and that knowledge was worth the price of a thousand admissions.

Colleen X understood she would soon be facing parental punishment, but as Hector held her hand and walked her home in real twilight, the fulfillment of stars she had long wished upon now made her a young woman forever changed.

NAMOR

BY J. ANTHONY ROMAN

My lease is about to expire, and I'm not sure what I'm going to do. If I re-sign, my rent goes up to the point that it will be vital for me to earn an income, no more passion work. My home is part of my very being and my workplace.

I grew up in the Mott Haven section of the Bronx. *"The Mott Haven section of the Bronx."* I say it like that because it's how all the newscasters used to announce it when they were reporting on whatever drug-related, multiple murder happened that day. I'm proud of where I'm from, but it doesn't agree with my soul. I left Mott Haven years ago and never looked back, at least not as an option for habitation.

Watching my mother's ability to sketch the faces of our family and the hands of praying saints, I picked up the habit of art. My family supported that, and it evolved into graphic design. I used being an artist as my main excuse for leaving the hood. I mean I had to be closer to work, so that meant downtown Manhattan. I found a nice sublet on the east side, and eventually took over the lease. I currently have half-a-career as a freelance graphic designer.

I have this really cool client whose porn site I work on, and he's one of the few I can stand being around when I'm not charging them by the hour. We're throwing them back and I tell him my story, and he's like "Bro, you're like Namor the Sub-Mariner"

That is, *the* Namor the Sub-Mariner, created in 1939, by artist and writer Bill Everett. Namor was what happened when a human sea captain seduced a princess from Atlantis, creating Marvel Universe's first mutant. Often confused with DC's Aquaman, Namor has a fully amphibious physiology, super strength, speed, a pair of wings on his ankles, and what truly legitimizes him as a marvel, the ability to fly.

Namor suffers from biological duality. Humans are scared and jealous of him because of his abilities.

The Atlantians, although they recognize his regality and power, know that he is not a purebred, and the other half of him happens to belong to the race that's destroying their environment. Half-human, half-Atlantian, never truly embraced anywhere. It's because of this Namor was always helping mankind one day, then attacking it the next.

I might have left the hood twenty years ago, but—thing is—the hood never leaves you. If you ever watch anyone who grew up during the depression operate a business, you'll know what I'm talking about. Poverty is a treacherous shadow that darkens your decisions with doubt. And whatever negative connotations I have about the hood, I have never let myself fully leave it. Even when I picked out the apartment on the east side, what tipped the scales was that it overlooked the George Washington Carver housing project.

It's a compulsion. When I first started graphic design, I sold weed to all my clients even though I didn't really have to. Made myself stop because they started treating me like a drug dealer, not like their graphic designer. That's the thing with people in this industry, once they know you're from the hood, and you sell them a little grass, you're just that kind of person to them. They're not willing to accept complexities, outside of their own work anyway. Frail, flaky, *industry* people. I don't even mingle with them anymore. I know it's bad for my wallet, but I just let my work do the talking. My dilemma? I could stand the people in the hood even less.

Before I go on with my tale, I should add that when the economy tanked in 2008, I eventually lost more than half of my clients. To fill the void I chose to get a 9 to 5 job. I wanted it to have nothing to do with design, so I would hunger for it all day and work harder at night. I took some tests, and became a certified lead inspector. Where am I working? The Bronx division of the New York City Housing Authority. Back to the hood.

Now I spend my days shit-stomping across the Bronx and dealing with tenants and my nights in front of a Mac putting up with clients.

I'm in Cafe Tallulah watching my client pick out the ugliest of my designs. Four hours earlier I was breaking up a fight in the Patterson projects breakroom.

I'm on the balcony of the Morgan Stanley building, overlooking Times Square at night, drinking this client's Chablis during a break, face-timing with an old classmate, bitching about how much more we like Photoshop over InDesign; that morning I was soaking wet from the rain, dressed in workman's blues and getting stuck in a piss-drenched elevator (yeah, that cliché is true).

I know I'm not part of either of these worlds, completely.

And now because of my good work ethic, I'm offered a promotion at the day job. I can even choose to live in the projects now because of the position I would have there. I could get a great check, and pay nothing, forever. I could shut down my graphic design company I worked so hard to build, and return to the Bronx, instead of constantly struggling to pay more rent to stay amongst the assholes I deal with daily.

So whatever happened to Namor? Since the Marvel Universe is an ongoing entity, his story doesn't really have an ending. But there are several strands about the future of this character, and one of the more popular and feasible comes from the Earth X story line. His biological duality causes dementia, and in this state, he kills Mr. Fantastic from the Fantastic Four. Mr. Fantastic's son, Franklin, witnesses this, and because he possesses the power to manipulate reality, he causes Namor to combust, burning half of his body, forcing him to live the rest of his life in permanent flame and pain.

I tossed a client's laptop out of his parked car the other day. He tried to stiff me on a payment; I knew it would scare him, and I knew his bitch ass wouldn't do shit back about his broken computer.

At the day job, I saw this group of kids, one of them wielding a semi-automatic, chasing another boy who ran into traffic and was hit by the BX15 on Willis Avenue.

After I saw it happen, I pulled out a marker and just started drawing. Everywhere. Even on cars. I got arrested when I reached a cop car.

In the overnight stay in prison, even in that solitude, I couldn't make up my mind about my apartment, my lease, and if I should renew. I just hoped it wouldn't hurt too much once the flames began to engulf my body.

THE CLEANING LADY

BY GIL FAGIANI

Solid as a hundred pound sack of rice, with short red hair, and walnut-colored skin, Belén lived alone in the same five-room apartment in the Melrose Houses project in the Bronx where she'd raised four daughters. One day, before the rooster's *ki-ki-ri-ki*—and there were roosters in her project— she woke up feeling frisky and decided to clean her apartment. She swept, vacuumed, and mopped all five rooms, and when finished sat down to have a cup of *café con leche* and read *el Diario*. She left one of the windows open and a warm breeze rippled the pages of the newspaper, reminding her that it was springtime. "*¡Coño—Damn!*" she said out loud, "It's time to do a *serious* spring cleaning!"

Opening her record cabinet, she pulled out some albums by Tito Rodríguez—Tito *Número Uno*, she called him—because she considered him superior to his musical rival Tito Puente. As soon as she heard Tito's voice and the horns and percussion of his orchestra, she kicked off her slippers, loosened her shoulders, and mamboed into her front closet. Using a mop handle as a partner, she dipped and turned while taking out buckets, mops, brushes, and soap. Starting with the rear bedroom, she washed the window panes, sills, and molding and scrubbed and waxed the floors. She had worked her way into the bathroom and was polishing the toilet when Paco called. He picked up that she was in a good mood and asked if he could stop by with some lunch.

"*¡Claro!—Sure!*" she said, "and bring some beer."

After pork sandwiches and a couple of Miller High Lifes, they ended up in bed. Paco was in his fifties and out of shape, but with the help of Belén's wildly undulating hips, he managed to pop his cork twice, something he hadn't done since he was a young man in the Army. Moaning softly, he'd just turned on his side and closed his eyes when Belén rolled out of bed, and came back with a washcloth.

"Clean up, papi, and then let me get back to my house cleaning." Paco would have preferred to linger for a while, but knowing how Belén got during one of her cleaning campaigns, he quickly got dressed and bolted out the door.

Putting on Tito Rodríguez's *Algo Nuevo—Something New*, Belén piled old newspapers, magazines, and empty bottles by her front door. In the process, she noticed a few dust balls and paper scraps on her floor, so she decided to sweep, vacuum, and mop her floors again, just for good measure.

Then she made another trip to the front closet, and pulled out a plastic bucket containing cloth rags, a feather-duster, a screwdriver, two pairs of white gloves, and a glass salt-shaker filled with cotton swabs. In her living room she feather-dusted her Puerto Rican tchotchkes: hand-painted maracas, ebony rhythm sticks, ceramic versions of *coquis*—Puerto Rican tree frogs—and her collection of miniature straw hats, huts and dolls. Next she dusted her furniture with the cotton rags and rubbed her wooden shelves with linseed oil. Taking a few deep breaths, Belén took the screwdriver and unscrewed the back panels of her radio and TV. Putting on a pair of white gloves, she dragged her index finger through the maze of tubes. Whenever her white finger became smudged with dirt, she used a cotton swab to carefully scour out the source of dust or grime.

She wanted in the worst way to take apart and dust all the light bulb fixtures in her apartment, but remembered once trying it and receiving an electric shock that caused her to fall off a stepladder and smash her knee. Even now, when the weather was damp, that knee was stiff and painful.

It was nine o'clock at night when it dawned on her that she really hadn't been as thorough as she should have been in throwing things out. She went back into her bedroom closets and pulled out jackets, dresses, blouses, and slacks she didn't wear anymore and dropped them on the floor. Next she went through her bureau drawers and did the same thing with her slips, bras, panties and socks, adding them to the growing pile in the middle of the floor.

Then she went into what had been her daughters' rooms. She kept a lot of their clothing, even though they were all married and had long-ago moved out. They rarely came by anymore and she figured she might as well bring the clothing down to the community room, where *los pobres*—the poor people—could benefit from them. In the back of a closet she noticed dolls, board games and toys of all kinds. She had hoped someday her grandchildren would have played with them. Nothing in life works out the way you want it, she thought, shaking her head. The toys were only collecting dust and attracting bugs. And indeed as she cleared them out of the closet she swore she could see snakelike clusters of dust, along with roach shells, mouse droppings and paint and plaster chips.

It was after midnight when she carted all the clothes and toys downstairs. The community room was unlit and locked, so as neatly as she could, she stacked the clothes and toys by the doorway. Once upstairs, she rummaged through her record collection and had just picked out an album of *boleros* by Tito *Número Uno*, when the telephone rang. It was her daughter Pura.

"Mami, I was in the neighborhood and saw your lights on, *¿Todo está bien?—Is everything OK?*"

"Don't worry about me, I'm O.K. But remember what I said the last time; I have no more money for your drug habit."

"*Coño*, mami, I told you I'm clean now. I went through a program."

Belén put the record she was holding on her turntable and began to dance slowly. Tito's broad, handsome face beamed from the album cover she held tightly to her breasts. "O.K.," Belén said, "I'm busy now . . ."

"Mami, talking about drugs, I hope you're . . ."

"I'll see you," Belén said, dropping the phone on the receiver.

Stretching her arms, Belén felt a surge of energy and with trembling hands, opened a kitchen window. The moon was full and its bright light illuminated her pinched face and protruding eyes. Suddenly she remembered the filth that she had uncovered in her closets and dragged the broom, dustpan, vacuum cleaner, mop and buckets back into the bedrooms. She was vacuuming a closet when she heard a muffled cry and the pounding of a stick against the ceiling of the apartment below. She ignored the sounds but in a few minutes the telephone rang.

"Who is it?" Belén asked.

"It's Carmen, your neighbor below. You woke up my husband. Can't you wait until tomorrow to do your damn vacuuming? *Por favor!*"

"Not all of us in this building are pigs. I've seen that good-for-nothing husband of yours throw beer cans out the window . . ."

"*Lies! . . . Maricona!*"

"You're the lying faggot! *¡Hija di gran puta!—Daughter of a big whore!*" Belén shouted, letting the phone dangle on its cord. She was really worked up now. Her mouth was dry and a white coating began to form in the corner of her lips. That's the problem with this neighborhood, she told herself. Too many pigs, and too little cleanliness. Images of dead dogs in alleyways, water bugs, rats, roaches, blackened carcasses of cars, and mountains of empty tin cans passed through her mind.

She still had it in her head there was too much clutter in her apartment and rushed into her bathroom with a plastic garbage bag. She threw in half-used shampoo, conditioner, and perfume bottles. Opening her medicine cabinet she scooped out a half a dozen smoky brown vials of pills, spilling their contents on the tile floor.

"*¡Coño!*" she said, running for a dustpan and brush, but then remembering she hadn't finished cleaning the bedrooms yet.

It was three o'clock in the morning when she realized that she had tracked white powder all over her apartment from the pills she had stepped on in her bathroom. Sweat poured down her face and her lips looked sugarcoated. She couldn't stop moving and put on another Tito Rodríguez album, this one featuring cha'-cha'-cha' favorites from Cuba. The woman below continued to bang her broomstick on the ceiling and there was a heavy pounding on her front door. "*¡Epa!* " Belén shouted, as she threw her arms in front of her like she was squeezing a dance partner and cha'-cha'-cha'-ed towards the howling vacuum cleaner.

The next evening Belén shuffled stiffly in an aqua green gown down Ward 9 at Bronx State Hospital. She stared straight ahead, her lips cracked, not saying a word to anyone. Listed in the hospital records as a multiple admission, the staff nicknamed her The Cleaning Lady, and except for insisting that she take her meds, left her alone. Inside a visiting room filled with cigarette smoke and cockroaches, Paco and Pura sat around a plastic table with an uneaten container of rice and chicken Pura had cooked for her mother.

Belén had been brought in earlier in the day by the police. As the sun came up, she started throwing her cleaning equipment out the window: brooms, dust pans, vacuum cleaner, mops, buckets, rubber gloves, detergent, furniture polish, and cleaning rags. Then she let it fly with her Tito Rodríguez albums, cracking the window of a neighborhood bodega below. One of the cops who forced his way into her apartment said she was foaming at the mouth like a rabid dog, and screaming, *"¡Qué viva Tito Número Uno!"* when they handcuffed her and drove her to the hospital.

HOOK

BY RON KOLM

What the *fuck*!" Duke muttered, amazed at what he was seeing in the darkened bookstore. A thin curtain of smoke was rising from under the baseboard like an inverted waterfall. It stretched the entire length of the left wall.

Holy shit, the joint's on *fire*! I better get the fuck out of here, he thought, turning back towards the bathroom window he'd just busted to get in. But then he noticed something odd—the smoke smelled like marijuana—one of his favorite things— so he hesitated a moment—and then he became aware of the pounding and shaking—it felt like a humongous semi grinding down St. Mark's Place in second gear.

And, finally, he picked up on the sounds; shouting, cursing, music (Duke had problems with his hearing—*way* too much heavy metal over the years).

"Jesus, must be some kinda weird party or something goin' on next door," Duke said, thinking out loud while lighting a stray joint he found in his pocket. He was curious and, anyway, he could always come back later to clean the place out—so Duke hoisted himself through the splintered window frame and dropped down onto the bare plot of ground behind the bookstore.

The space next to the East Village Bookstore had been converted into a unisex haircutting boutique: HAIRPOWER TO THE PEOPLE. It had a couple of windows in the rear wall, so Duke eased over to check things out.

"Man, world's totally fuckin' nuts!" he whistled. All the furniture had been piled against the walls and the front grates had been lowered. Bathed in unnaturally bright light, a bunch of Hell's Angels, dressed in full colors, were slow-dancing with the male hairdressers.

One of the Angels seemed to be holding a metallic object; light glinted on it brightly. Duke squinted, trying to determine if it was a gun or a knife—but it turned out to be neither. This particular Angel had a mechanical hook for a hand and, in thrall to the music, he pressed it deeply into the small of his partner's back.

Now Duke remembered. He'd seen this guy hanging out on St. Mark's Place, hassling passing tourists. The Angel would use his hook as bait, attracting the naive, the curious and the stupid, engage them in conversation, turn it strange, get pissed off and then beat the unsuspecting victim to a pulp with his steely contraption.

Duke winced—not his idea of a good time. He turned to re-enter the bookstore just as the music changed. The slow song segued into the raucous chords of the Dead Kennedys' "Too Drunk to Fuck," and the partygoers began to slam into each other like battered cars in a demolition derby.

Duke couldn't help himself—he started pogoing spastically—and that was his undoing. One of the Angels noticed his pale countenance bobbing up and down outside the window. He let out a yell, directing all eyes towards the back of the barbershop. Everyone froze—and then, as if at a hidden command, an angry horde of sweaty, drug-crazed psychopaths charged the back door.

Duke frantically jumped at a fire escape ladder dangling just above his head and managed to grab hold of the bottom rung. He pulled his skinny, drug-wasted body up by sheer will alone. The Angel with the hook took a swipe at Duke's disappearing leg, snagging a strip of already frayed jeans.

***

The hot, noonday sun beat down on a frazzled Duke. He was squatting against the blue, cinder block wall of the St. Mark's Cinema, very broke and totally stoned. Somehow he was gonna have to figure out another way to rip off the bookstore across the street—man, there was only *one* fucking clerk running the whole joint—that's *practically* an open invitation—shit, hitting a place like that *should* be as easy as *taking a crap*.

Doing the bathroom window again at night was flat out. Earlier in the day he'd seen a couple of repair guys with toolboxes and armloads of two-by-fours go into the shop, followed by a lot of hammering and drilling.

Armed robbery was also out of the question—the cops had confiscated his gun—something about one of his friends getting blown away while playing Russian roulette with it.

Duke decided on the direct approach. He got up, crossed the street and stepped into the dank, ill-lit recesses of the bookstore. Books and pamphlets were casually strewn around on old wooden sale tables. Duke checked out the guy working at the front counter; a tall, long-haired dude with thick John Lennon granny glasses. The clerk seemed to be deeply engrossed in an underground comic—*Zap* #4, Duke guessed from the cover.

This'll be like taking candy from a fuckin' baby, he thought, walking back towards the very bathroom he'd broken into last night. To the right of the bathroom was a small messy office, created by mass-market display racks jutting out from the wall. Duke sidled in behind the makeshift barrier.

Inside, a half-eaten sandwich adorned a chipped wooden desk, next to tumbled stacks of indecipherable ledgers. A battered bicycle was chained to one of the legs. Duke simply tilted the desk back and slipped the lock free. Yeah, he'd take the bike—it had *real* value—not like those fucking *books*—you had to heist so *many* of them to make it worth your while.

He rummaged through the desk looking for cash, but came up empty. Duke shrugged, stuffed the sandwich in his pocket and wheeled the bike towards the exit.

Just as he was about to leave the premises, the bookstore clerk materialized in front of him—from out of thin air—blocking his path.

"Hey, man, what do you think you're *doing*? That doesn't *belong* to you. Please be cool and put it back," the apparition lectured. It was dressed in a faded tie-dyed T-shirt and ancient bell-bottoms. For sure *this* one don't live on the street, Duke thought.

"I really must ask you to *split*, or I'll be forced to call the police," the obstruction continued, grabbing the handlebars and attempting to wrest the bike from Duke.

That was a mistake. Duke popped the guy, knocking him to the floor.

"Get the *fuck* out of my way, asshole—I *hate* old hippies," Duke snarled, pushing the bicycle out of the store. He looked back to see if the clerk was going to try to get up and follow him, and felt the bike bump into something—or someone. Duke whirled around and found himself face to face with the one-armed Angel (the tourist he'd been messing with gladly fled).

"I remember *you*," the Angel gloated, raising his hook.

UPPER WEST TO LOWER EAST

BY MICHAEL GATLIN

Sezso Ximenez carefully opens the window. He crawls out onto the fire escape and closes it from the outside. He has been doing this for years—slipping out into the night without so much as a suspicious knock on his bedroom door from any member of his family.

He is the man of the house, the provider, the king. The nighttime is his time. He is an explorer of the late hours.

He is happy his birthday is over. Sezso hates the songs, the cake, the arbitrary presents that aren't wanted, and the worst . . . aging—the melatonin going, the testosterone fading . . .

Two black tennis shoes hit the sidewalk softly as Sezso lands from the last rusted steel rung of the fire escape. He is free from his known life as a faux paternal, familial and financial provider. Free from the presence of his family home. He escapes into the wild Manhattan jungle in search of a medium.

Sezso glides through the streets in black pants and shirt. No one notices him as he slinks quickly down the sidewalk.

He finds his surface: A brick wall on Chrystie Street. Sezso unrolls a six-foot stencil slowly, spraying black paint as he goes. His rubber gloves quickly darken. The stencil is of a Catholic priest in full vestments. The priest is giving communion; the host outstretched from his holy offering. Sezso uses only black on the priest. He quickly rolls the stencil up.

He finds another stencil in his backpack, a kneeling clown. He paints yellow as he unrolls. This stencil is beside and beneath the priest. The clown extends his tongue receiving the holy wafer. He then tapes up a holey stencil to cover the clown suit with polka-dots. He sprays the dots blue, then outlines the shape and features of the face in blue. Sezso tapes up another stencil and sprays the clown nose and hair red.

The clown has a much exaggerated red smile and open mouth, tongue extended. His hands are clasped in front of his belly, below the offering host, around a single reed bulb horn; the kind Harpo Marx spoke with. There is tension and comedy in the piece. The communion will be exaggerated by a slapstick noise.

Sezso rerolls the stencil scrolls and removes his rubber gloves. The contraband is hidden in his back-pack, black and snug against his frame as he disappears into the shadows.

Sezso Ximenez is half Mayan Indian and half Spanish Conquistador: His great-to-the-whatever grandfather on his father's side was aboard Cortes' ship of gold hunting soldiers who killed savages thoroughly while searching for the map to El Dorado. His great-to-the-whatever grandfather on his mother's side was a Quichean warrior from Guatemala and survived for many generations and many wars and had many children. Sezso discovered this when he was nine years old and his father had encouraged the young prodigy to do a family tree for his mother.

At the age of twelve Sezso created the family tree of his father and the family tree of his mother. He spent two weeks on the Internet researching ancient connections. He presented the two five-by-three-foot trees to his parents for their fifteenth wedding anniversary.

The trees were done in accurate browns and detailed greens and enlisted the names of hundreds and hundreds of relatives. It was the first time he saw his father cry because of something that he had made. This one act turned Sezso into an artist.

His father studied the trees intently. He had them both framed and they rested on the ground by their bed. Three years later, he was gone, lost to the furies of the Atlantic Ocean.

Sezso's father was a fisherman. His boat capsized. He became part of the sea. His flesh dissolved and was consumed and transformed with his bones and fluids and tissue to the purity of the carbon element. He was indeed no more.

Before he left the earth, Sezso's father taught him to catch, scale and cook fish. They would walk from their Upper West Side apartment on Saturdays through Riverside Drive Park to the docks where Franklin's father parked his fishing boat. It seemed enormous to Sezso then, in the glorious sun, with the dirty water lapping against the old wooden docks.

Sezso's mother, Ramona Ximenez, was in shock when she realized that they had saved very little money and that she was going to have to not only work but move her family from the safe Upper West Side to the dangerous Lower East Side of Manhattan: riches to rags, practically overnight. Sezso was also in shock and spoke to no one for a year.

Today, Ramona Ximenez is a 250-pound ultra-hyper helicopter-mom whose sole desire in life is to cook, clean, and take care of her four children, which she does with suffocating gusto. Her large Paleolithic-Venus breasts have enough milk to feed an entire housing complex in the projects where she lives with her children: Sezso, Juanez, Manuelo, and Ivana.

Ivana is a gorgeous fourteen-year-old blossom who fears the world away from her mother's girth and stink of birth. She will be a woman soon and is ready to leave the house, get married, get pregnant, and get tied to the kitchen life, which is the way it has always been in their family.

Manuelo is twelve, and is already starting to drink, smoke pot, and steal petty items from small stores. Neither he nor his sister remembers their father at all.

Juanez is nineteen, and has just been accepted into college.

Ramona insists that Sezso help her raise his three remaining siblings and pay for his sister and brother's school before he moves out of their four-bedroom apartment on Norfolk.

She is terrified that when her children move out she will be left alone. She shackles her kids to her apron strings with a loving noose designed to tighten anytime they get a sniff of the outside world. Sezso has to go out and make a living—she understands that—but she begs him to continue to live at home for as long as he can, *to help with Ivana and Manuelo.* She says Juanez is already a man—beyond her parental control.

Sezso has had to fight his whole life because of his very attractive and very feminine good looks. His thin dark face with its perfectly manicured goatee, razor cheeks, thick lashes, smoldering milk chocolate eyes drove the girls in the neighborhood crazy, and the boys in the hood cracked him in the jaw every once in a while—as if trying to prove that they were the better mating choice.

During the day Sezso earns money as a game programmer—enough money to support his entire family though his siblings are unaware of this fact. They wonder sometimes why he hasn't left the house and started his own family. What else can he do? His mother begs him to stay and he stays. Stays and pays for groceries and his siblings' education.

Sezso often thinks of his father. He remembers the big fisherman who loved the boat and the ride of the sea. He remembers what a prize occasion it was each and every one of the four times he actually went out to sea with him.

The first time he had just turned nine and the experience was terrifying. The waves were particularly rough for such a partly-cloudy day and the only thing he remembers is throwing up in the cabin for hours.

The second time he was eleven. This was supposed to make Sezso a man, but he was still going to getting beaten up at school most days because he was having frequent erection attacks and his classmates had started calling him "boner." On this journey Sezso didn't vomit, but he didn't fish either. He was too terrified to let go of the railing.

The third time on his father's boat, Sezso fished. He was fourteen. He dropped the line into the water and let it explore the ocean depths. He caught a fish that day: one fish—a ten pound baby bass. It was enough to make his father proud.

On his fifteenth birthday Sezso flung the line further, baited it with larger prey, meatier chunks. He was stronger that year, muscles now formed around his svelte brown frame, hair fuzzed his legs and arms and his facial hair was darker, more noticeable.

Suddenly, Sezso hooked a three hundred pound shark. His father watched the rippling muscles on his son Sezso's body, his biceps pop and forearms flex as he tried to grip the reel. He watched the pole bend and stretch and knew instantly the boy had a monster. He didn't think the boy had a chance.

"Give me the line son."

"No! *I* caught him!"

Diego Ximenez stepped back, challenged by his son for the first time. He felt so proud, he almost cried. It did not matter to him that the boy might not be able to reel in the fish.

Sezso took a deep breath and struggled with the mightiest force he had ever encountered. He was in his first year of high school and on the varsity base-ball team. He was exercising most of his erections away and learning to size up his classmates as friend, lover, or foe. He thought he had it all figured out until he hooked this fish.

He pulled and tugged. He wrapped his inexperienced hands around the line and cut his left hand wide open: blood. He kept gripping the pole, fighting the fish, turning the crank, dripping with blood. He wasn't getting off of the boat without that fish.

That was the day everything changed for Sezso. That eighty-degree day in the perfect blue waters, blue sky with nothing to do but battle nature, god, and the self in one long marathon struggle to catch a bucking fish.

Sezso still had the original photograph and newspaper article of the young man and his father. In the photograph, Sezso posed with the three hundred pound shark that gave him an epic two-hour battle that he eventually won. It was such a beautiful day.

Now, in the cool early June night of another year, Sezso Ximenez smokes a cigarette on the fire-escape, and thinks about his life since then. He hopes his sister isn't watching.

She is.

Ivana can hear the very silent Sezso when he opens the window. She loves it when she hears him come home. She can finally sleep then. No one knows why her grades suffer and she is tired all of the time. She watches the glamorous cigarette smoke flow from her brother's mouth and nose in silhouette rivers behind her room's thin blinds. She hopes it will not be a long night.

Sezso puts out his cigarette and dashes out into the evening, down the ninja fire-escape and soft onto the sidewalk. He has work to do, scores to settle with the way it is and the way it should be.

The playground at night is a still masterpiece of silence. The chains do not squeak with swinging children, pulling and kicking limbs with laughter, swinging to the absolute highest point possible before exhaustion or jumping, depending on the bravery and will of the child. The slides reflect moonlight in their chrome tongue offering, twisting in scooped spirals, rising and falling in humped length, landing in a pit of sand where children either pillow or stick a landing. The monkey bars are simple skeletons of unfurnished homes, indestructible jail-cells, or domes of iron wrought for training exercise only.

It is three in the morning. Sezso's shadow drifts across the playground. He slithers along the walls and dark corners, until he shows himself, running across the court, dribbling an imaginary basketball, cutting and slicing as if he is playing a game with a team of invisible competitors. Near the hoop, he leaps high to dunk the imaginary ball, and holds onto the rim. With incredible strength pulls himself up, straddles the rim and leans against the backboard, then attaches a brand new rope basketball net to the naked steel circle. This is one of his favorite hobbies.

When he was younger—ten, eleven, twelve—Sezso loved to hear the swoosh of the basketball net when he played. The onomatopoeic *SwWOoosh*—filling him with the sense of accomplishment with a sound like windy silk.

Sezso smiles as he finishes attaching the final loop. He drops to the ground, soft shoes silent on the asphalt court. He returns to the shadows, disappearing in the concrete darkness with the ease of a tomcat.

He skips in and out of the parking lots and parks and playgrounds around Manhattan dressing one hundred nets on one hundred naked rims and inventing the realities of a hundred success stories that end with the same sound: *SwWOoosh!*

He scores three hundred points from impossible distances; shooting one hundred times and making every one. He is the all-time leading scorer in the Ghost League and no one knows his secret.

IMITATIONS OF CHRIST

BY PETER MARRA

And her bloodstained kiss burned my lips...

You may have heard other versions of this story. But this is the straight shit.

They didn't hold me in stir very long. After the incident of two days ago, I was kept on ice at Manhattan South in a cell with a couple of wholesome guys who would give me the once over every so often, after breakfast and after lunch. They would look me up and down, and sensuously lick their lips in unison. I pretty much expected to become their girlfriend, but surprisingly nothing ever happened. I guess they were a little put off by the reason that I was there in the first place. Rumors precede you in prison.

The cops, despite their best efforts, couldn't produce a corpse. When they arrived at the diner that afternoon they found me, a catatonic waitress in the corner, and a pool of coagulating blood on the floor. One of the cops, a dumb fat fuck, slipped on the blood, fell right onto his greasy pig ass and couldn't get up. When his partners helped him up he puked and they laughed. The waitress was transported to Bellevue, she's still there and from what I've heard, she will remain there for a very long time counting her fingers over and over again.

They let me out around 5 p.m.—no hard evidence. Also, my inalienable rights had been violated, they had forgotten the Miranda, and so I walked. It was December and the sky was a black velvet painting: faces stretched taut across the sky, a handful of stars, a twinkle, and a flash every so often. I headed to the last comfortable place I could think of: A diner on Eighth Avenue near Forty-third Street, near the old Show World Sex Emporium, now a haunted house entertainment dump for the tourists. As always I was drawn to Times Square, even when it was just to watch it die in a pool of sewer water choking on its own blood and vomit.

The diner I am referring to was never touched by the march of progress. The windows were eternally greasy. When I entered, I was assaulted by a wall of cigarette smoke, bacon grease, and human stink. Formica circa '65 completed a scene populated with a collection of rancid hookers and scabby drunks teetering on wooden chairs. One junkie, post-main-line, was attempting to eat a hamburger deluxe, but could never get it together enough to take a bite. His eyes rolled back, his lids drooped, his mouth missed the burger and his head gradually inched closer to his french fries and ketchup until at the last possible second his neck would snap back and like Sisyphus, he would start all over again.

I saw that an old acquaintance, Criselda, was working behind the counter. This was a lucky break. I approached the counter; she smiled when she recognized me.

"Hey baby! What's up?" She shook her head when I finished my story. "Assholes! You're a dumb motherfucker! How does this shit happen to you all the time?"

"Anyway," I shrugged, "I need a weapon."

"Sure, papi." She reached under the counter, pulled out a brown paper bag and handed it over. I looked around quickly, a little nervous that people might notice.

"Don't worry about these assholes! Bunch of drugged out cunts and dicks. Fuckups," she said. "Here! Take it. Blued steel, the number's been filed off. Can't be traced. Pay me when you have the money."

"Thanks. Can you get me a black coffee too?"

She gave me the black coffee and I went to sit by the front window at a rickety table which I steadied with a couple of folded napkins placed under one leg. I was glad I ran into her. The word on the street was that she was expert in the Tarot and also possessed a vagina with teeth, which she had used to murderous advantage in the past. I wouldn't know, but there was that nasty incident at the peep show in Coney Island years ago, all that blood and several dead johns, but the evidence didn't stick and she walked. Cris bore an uncanny resemblance to 1940s film icon Maria Montez, which made her all the more endearing.

I opened the bag under the table, took the piece out, gave it a quick once over: Smith & Wesson snub nose .38 Special Model 10, blued steel like Criselda had promised. I hid it in my coat pocket. My girl always came through in a pinch.

I stared out the window at the Church across the street. A seagull perched on the top of the steeple's cross collapsed and fell several stories, ending with a splat on the pavement. It just lay there. An old man stopped to stand over the bird and inspect it. As he looked at the bird, two passing youths knocked the nosey old fart down and robbed him. As he lay on the ground, they kicked him in the head exactly three times. He shook a little then stopped. The kids ran away. Then the bird moved, stood up, teetered, and flew off. A fucking miracle. The old codger remained comatose. People came. People went. Time marched on. He bled. Eventually the cops showed up.

"Nice hustle," I thought. I felt the fear coming on and headed out the door, making my way to the subway. My stomach was flipping, my balls were rising into my gut, and my hands and feet ached. There was a small circle of blood in each palm. This was not the time for the stigmata. At the corner, I heard the distant groan of a female voice. I shoved my hands into my pockets. Resisting the urge to turn around and see who was moaning, I crossed the street to the subway entrance and made my way down the stairs into the filth and fury of the station. Finally, a place where I felt less nervous. A place of queasy comfort.

The E train to Queens pulled in and I got on. The train was crowded and I had to stand. A few feet away from me I noticed an exhausted Hispanic woman, about forty, holding herself up with great effort. She was in front of an old woman who was nodding off in her seat. At the Lexington Avenue-Fifty-third street stop, the old lady toddled off and before the exhausted Hispanic woman could sit down, a 16-year-old kid with shorts that ended just below the knees slipped in and took the seat. He looked like a real arrogant prick. She was furious.

"Wonderful! Thanks for stealing the seat, ass-hole!" she screamed.

The kid started babbling in Spanish. I don't know Spanish very well but I detected the word *puta*. "You motherfucker," she screamed, spit flying every-where, "You know what's gonna happen now fucker?! At the next stop I'm gonna drag you off this fuckin' train, arrest you and shove this fuckin' badge right up your skinny faggot ass! Then I'm gonna rip your tiny balls off and shove them in your mouth!"

Upon saying this she produced what looked like a NYC shield. Fuck, she was a cop. She then pro-ceeded to shove the badge in the youth's face so hard that his nose started bleeding.

"You gonna cry faggot? Sure, start crying you little piece of shit." He was fighting back tears, humiliated. This woman was upset. At the next stop the kid slid out of the seat and ran out the door, like the devil was trying to bite his ass. She sat down, smoothed her hair and smiled. Several other people got off next and I was able to sit right next to her, making sure my gun was well hidden. I was nervous, but in a strange way she fascinated me.

A couple of more stops went by; she turned to look at me.

"You a private investigator?" she asked. "You look like it."

"Sort of."

"You either are or you ain't."

"Then, the answer is 'yes.'"

"Mr. Fuckin' Secret Asshole," she snapped.

She gave off a weird vibe. We rode on in silence until we hit the Roosevelt Avenue station.

"Wanna come?" she said. I nodded yes, we got off.

"Where are we goin'?" I asked.

"Shut the fuck up and come with me."

We walked up the stairs and got out on Seventy-fourth Street. She took my hand and almost dragged me down Roosevelt Avenue.

"Ow! Ow! Fuck! You're hurting my hand." She was digging her nails into my wrist.

"Stop whining!"

We stopped in front of a dive with the word "Romanticos" emblazoned in purple neon. Underneath the sign was the afterthought "A gentleman's club" in red neon script. I laughed when I saw that.

"Romanticos? This place is a shithole!"

She shoved me inside.

The place smelled like cigarette smoke, grease and puke. There was a shitty little bar and there was a broken-ass stage in the back, upon which a topless broken-ass dancer was gyrating to extremely loud salsa music. Her g-string was soiled and I was close enough to see she had dirt under her fingernails. Her rat's nest blonde hair was greasy. Watching her were three bored men who briefly glanced at us. Yeah, that's it guys: Romanticos. Tiny black things were scurrying across the beat up linoleum floor.

My date brought us to a table near the stage and motioned to me to sit down. I sighed and took a seat. She sat down and lit a cigarette, blowing the blue smoke into the air. It hung for a second. I checked that my sidearm was secure. I could see that the dancer was starting to get tired and limp.

"Why are we here?" I asked.

"I come here to relax after work. Couple of times a week. Usually by myself. I live upstairs, so it's a short trip home."

The progression to decay happens too quickly. The neon clock that hung over the rat-ass-faced barmaid said it was 9:09 p.m. I was regretting my decision to talk to her on the subway.

"Would you like something to drink?" I asked her. She shook her head no.

"They'll let us sit here," she said, "I come here often. They won't complain."

I decided a shot was in order and got some Maker's Mark at the bar. When I came back, I noticed her hands fumbling under the table. Got me nervous. Real nervous.

"What are you doing?"

She pulled her hands from underneath the table. In her trembling fingers was a rosewood rosary, the beads worn smooth. I felt nauseous and sad. Bad images.

"Do you pray? Do you have any religious beliefs?" she asked.

"No, not after spending twelve years in Catholic school. That shit burned me good."

I described my memories to her of a nun I had as a teacher in the fifth grade: Sister Theresa. It was 1969, when the Vatican changed the nuns' outfits because everyone had become so hip. The dresses (or habits as they were officially called) became shorter, ending right on the knees and the head-gear (or wimple) was modified so that the hair was visible. Anyway, Sister Theresa was blessed with a voluptuous pneumatic body that didn't stop and she had beautiful crimson hair that cascaded to her shoulders. I remember sitting in class daydreaming about what her bush looked like, if it matched the hair on her head—if it was a flaming triangle of a moist soul that offered eternal redemption, a maximum overdrive climax for my nascent sex cravings.

After I finished childhood reminiscence, my companion made a quick sign of the cross. I gulped back my drink. Went up and got another.

"Can I see the gun you've been carrying?" she asked when I returned.

"I have no gun."

"You're not hiding the piece very well, give it here. Let me see it or I'll bust you. I really am a cop."

"I know. I saw that incident between you and the kid."

"Yeah, I feel bad about it. He's my son."

"Bullshit. I don't believe you.'

She rummaged in the left hand pocket of her blazer and produced a very worn photograph. She flipped it over to me. It was the same kid, standing in front of a house. He looked a little younger, maybe it was him. She had forgotten about my gun.

"He lives on the street. I kicked him out last year. He's no good. Still, It hurts me. The mirror cracked. He can't see himself no more."

I could see one bare tear in the corner of her right eye. It oozed out and trickled down her cheek. She allowed me to hold her hand, which made the both of us smile. After a few minutes she yanked it back and I could see her stiffen.

"I think you better get outta here. Get the fuck out," she whispered.

I took her advice and walked to the door. Once outside, I saw Criselda leaning against a beat up mustang right in front of the bar. She slowly shook her head.

"I followed you here. You and that gun were meant for trouble."

"Don't worry, nothing happened." I felt for my gun. My pockets were empty.

"Fuck! The piece you sold me is gone. She must have taken it." I knew I couldn't get it back without making a scene that would end in disaster.

At that moment I heard two short familiar pops. Gunshots. The door behind me flew open and I could hear a commotion inside Romanticos. The dancer, still topless, ran out screaming. Her face, contorted in fear, was covered in blood, an exquisite mask in the moonlight.

"Please, please!! She shot herself! Please!" the dancer wailed at everyone, at anyone who would listen. People started to gather, several pulled out phones to call 911.

Criselda grabbed my elbow and said in a low voice, "Just walk away with me, don't run."

We made our way quickly to the corner. When we turned the corner, Cris moved in and kissed me. Salty white heat.

"You never save them, do you Max baby?" she asked.

"They have a choice," I said, looking down.

"Go. Don't stop," she whispered. "I'm going back. I have to tidy things up again for you. It's my job."

She turned around and quickly walked away, never looking back at me, as I had hoped she would.

I could hear the fading rapid click clack of her heels as she turned the corner.

I watched as the glare of the moon swallowed her.

I watched as the night devoured the day.

COMPASSION

BY JOANIE HIEGER FRITZ ZOSIKE

Nearly midnight. A knock at the door. I wasn't expecting any visitors. "Who is it?" I hate it when people come by unannounced and generally, don't even deign to answer.

"It's your neighbor, Mitchell."

The cast changed frequently in this old East Village tenement, but I hadn't known of any Mitchells to pass through its halls.

"Who?"

"Mitchell," the voice insisted.

"I don't know any Mitchell," I said, opening the door with little hesitation.

I grew up in Southern California. I was a welcoming fool. I couldn't adequately defend such a cavalier attitude here in New York City, but there was no one else here to restrain me, so no defense necessary, thank goodness.

A thin, disheveled man I didn't recognize stood in the hallway. "Man, I have to get to the hospital immediately. I'm burning up with fever. I'm sorry. I'm very sick from AIDS." I saw he was sweaty and shivery, and weren't those a couple of KS lesions on his face? He stood on the cold tile floor of the hallway in his stocking feet. Well, I thought, he could be very sick. He could simply be shoeless. Or maybe he's jonesing for dope.

Despite my doubts, I could easily see this Mitchell of a man was suffering. I asked him in and gave him a glass of water—in a plastic cup (let's not throw caution to the wind altogether). He sat on the edge of a folding chair in my kitchen, shivering and sniffling. I tried to stand by patiently until he was able to explain to me what the hell he wanted from a total stranger at this hour of night.

When he calmed down a bit, I offered to call an ambulance or a friend for him. "There's no need for you to do that," he said. "My lover John—he lives upstairs in Apartment 5C—He's working right now in Jersey, but if you could just lend me $21.75, I could take a cab to my own hospital near where I live in the Bronx. I'll see you get the money right back. Tonight," he promised.

I was confused by the specificity of the taxi fare. Did he take taxis to the Bronx often? He didn't look the type. And the exactness about when I would be repaid. Tonight? It's nearly midnight. Could he have maybe meant tomorrow night?

I was caught in a torrent of imagined dialogue. In one ear, a jaded New Yorker heckles, "You're being hustled. In the other kinder ear, a goodwill gremlin suggests, "But who would stage such an extraordinary scene in order to extort money from a neighbor?"

"He's not your neighbor," said my auntie in California.

"He's not being totally honest," said my alter ego, who doesn't want to think the worst of him, and yet the story was, well . . . a little absurd.

"He's a junkie," said the sour New Yorker with an all-knowing hiss.

Meanwhile, the face of every friend who lived with or had died of AIDS paraded in front of me. "Can't you see the KS lesions? Can't you see he's got the AIDS face? Didn't you notice he has the AIDS ass?

He's shivering. He's sweating. He's shaking. He can barely stand. Look how thin he is!" They continued parading before me with questioning faces, and they held up a sign bearing a single word: Compassion.

Enough already! Bunch of Jewish mothers.

I gave Mitchell the $21.75. Then I gave him an additional $20.25 for good measure.

"Oh, my God! Thank you . . . thank you . . . don't know how to thank you."

"Don't thank me. It's okay."

"No, really. I promise, you'll get your money back. You'll see."

I ignored the flutter. I just wanted him to leave and get well.

To be neighborly, I hung out with him until he pulled himself together enough for the long trip uptown. The whole time he regaled me with details of his difficult life. I nodded, "Uh-huh, uh-huh, uh-huh," thinking about a very late dinner and the comfortably numbing television fest to follow. Then my mind wandered farther afield.

I found myself hoping, perversely, the guy was truly critically ill. I yearned for him to keep burning up with fever; maybe even get worse, until he absolutely had to get to the hospital immediately. I preferred to see this unfortunate stranger in desperate straits rather than face the possibility that he was a fraud.

"It's okay, Mitchell. You'll get better. Things'll get better. Maybe you'll be the one doing me the favor next time."

On the other hand, perhaps what he really needed were his shoes to walk home to the Bronx. I imagined he came downtown to cop and was given an ultimatum. First he had to buy those selfsame shoes back from the dude above me on the fourth floor, the dealer who kicked his sorry butt downstairs with brutal threats: "I'm keeping your shoes right here till you get that bread, motherfucker."

In my mind's beta reel, I heard poor Mitchell being shoved up against the wall. "I don't care if you go door *(SLAP)* by *(SLAP)* door *(SLAP)* to every apartment in this fucking *(SLAP)* build *(SLAP)* ing *(SLAP)*. I don't care if you rob the corner *(SLAP)* deli *(SLAP)* or pick *(SLAP)* pocket *(SLAP)* some yuppie *(SLAP)* cocksucker *(SLAP)* going to a club on the Bowery *(SLAP)*. Get me my money any way you can, faggot *(SLAP)*, and do it quick *(SLAP)*—or else."

What kind of a scene did my mind need to write for him that would elicit my belief in him? And would it still be possible for me to emerge from this scene as an exemplary sister of human kindness? As "she who took the stranger into her home, despite his being a carrier of the dreaded plague . . . and possibly a weapon?"

Would I be cast as "The She," a beautiful, beneficent angel who gave him water, money and succor; who held him gingerly to her shoulder as he wept . . .

"I mean after all, Mitchell, who do we human beings have if we don't have each other?"

In order for this poor unfortunate man to be worthy of my selfless words of compassion, it seemed I had to condemn him to a dreadful disease or stultifying addiction—and force him to get bitch-slapped. It didn't matter to me, as I long as I came out smelling like a keeper of the roses rather than the archangel of condemnation.

I grew disgusted with myself. Obviously the guy was suffering, but that didn't necessarily make me a better person because I was reluctantly being nice to him. . . . Honestly. . . . I used to believe that caring for one's fellow human being was not foolhardy, that a communitarian impulse could be trusted without cynical afterthought or the need for recognition. Then why, in the pit of my stomach, was there still a cauldron of cold rage and fear—fear that I'd been taken for a naïve creampuff?

"Thank you, thank you so much. I'll never forget you."

Oh, so what if I was being deceived! Should that henceforth impede my natural impulse to be kind and open? Would it ultimately reduce my intelligence if I was, indeed, a bit of a giving fool?

"Really, it's cool. Just get better real soon."

"I will, I promise you, I will."

"Good," I said it and I meant it. . I blinked back tears and opened the door.

"Just . . . " he said, turning toward me before he departed. "Can you do me one last favor?"

Okay, I thought. Here we go. Is he going to pull a gun on me? Call up to his junkie buddies on the fourth floor to come on down and rip off my thread-bare apartment? Is this the part where he turns into an alien?

"Wha' . . . " I stammered, confused by my feverish ruminations. I gulped for air. "What?"

"Can I come back and see you when I'm better?" Mitchell asked sweetly.

In that moment, I was convinced that it really didn't matter whether Mitchell was a person living with AIDS or some poor bastard strung out on bad drugs—or both. In truth, it matters very little to whom you are kind. It simply matters that you *are* kind—and that you make a practice of giving with an undivided heart.

That's the key . . . undivided. The practice is the giving of loving-kindness. Allowing in your mind that loving-kindness still exists in this world.

Even if you live in New York City.

A PARK BENCH FOR TWO

BY PAUL SOHAR

An elderly gentleman in a raincoat, rather short but not bent in the back, enters Central Park from West Seventy-second Street. On his way to the plaza he sits down on a bench with a copy of *The New York Times* in his lap. The other end of the bench is already occupied by a young man wearing a pinstripe suit and a lavender Hello Kitty T-shirt. His legs are spread out in front and his arms are on the back of the bench, leaving little room for the newcomer. Although green is beginning to enliven the trees, it's a cloudy and coolish day, not ideal park weather. The usual parade of nannies with kids and strollers is not on. A quiet spot in a noisy city. Five minutes pass before the young man speaks without looking at his bench mate.

"Anything exciting in the paper?"

Silence. The traffic noise of Central Park West seems to come from another city in another land. The taxis honk, the buses buzz as they lumber out into the flow of cars, but these distant sounds have nothing to do with the park bench.

Finally the elderly gentlemen pipes up.

"It depends on what excites you."

First the young man nods to the park in general before he turns to face his bench partner.

"Anything more about the Incredible Shrinking Man?"

"Never heard of it."

"It was all over the news a couple of days ago. It seems, every morning this oldish gent, a frightened looking little geezer with a lot to worry about, he makes his appearance in a different corner of Central Park, dressed in nothing but a dirty old T-shirt and a pair of sneakers. And then he proceeds, with sincere earnestness, to display his shrinking part to every passerby, explaining how big it was in the arms of the night and even tries teasing it back to life. Didn't you read about it?"

"No," is the curt answer from the elderly gentleman.

"Obviously," the young man goes on, spinning the story in a leisurely way. "Obviously, the show attracts a few squealing nannies and the grinning park workers until the cops finally haul him off. By then he starts howling about the pills he gets in jail and how they fail to stop his incredible shrinking and by the next day, he says, he's no bigger than a rat, and why do you people want him to turn into that? Aren't there enough rats in the city already? He screams at the cops. And more, like: 'If not, then look at me now, take a good look before I fall through a sewer grate, and before you good folks blow up into huge balloons, filled with the fumes and farts of the streets . . . ' It was on TV, the show he puts on. I saw it the other night. Didn't you?"

"No."

"By then the nannies move on," the young man is undeterred by the lack of interest in his news item; it's like he's rehearsing for an audition. "Yes, the parade moves on, and only some professorial types on their way to the Museum stop to listen. 'Yea, big huge balloons,' he tells these suits passing by, 'And you and your briefcases will float out over the park and get punctured by the Empire State Building. And then you'll come down as empty sacks, you'll cover the whole City, bringing on the darkness of an endless night while I'll be safe in the sewers, protected by the sewer grates.' The scene ends with the cops throwing a tarp over him and escorting him out of the park. Wrapped in the unwieldy tarp he seems to shrink further but nowhere near the size of a rat when he gets shoved into a squad car. Only his voice never shrinks. 'Help, please somebody help me; they always make me shrink more in jail . . . ' You can hear his voice even over the police sirens. Well, what do you think? Is he going to be on *Oprah* next?"

This time the young man addresses the question directly into the elderly gentleman's face. The latter does not cringe but turns his wire-rimmed bifocals at him.

"Of course, he knows what he's doing. He knows we're living in an expanding universe, and he'll be back tomorrow and the day after, until he'll appear as a balloon in Macy's Thanksgiving Parade along with other icons of our infinitely varied civilization. After all, he seems to be commuting between the Met Museum and the Museum of Natural History, at least for now, until he has a museum of his own dedicated to his shrinking body."

The lines are delivered in the tone of an experienced salesman rather than that of a teacher. Then silence. The young man drops his broad shoulders on the back of the bench.

"You don't say."

"That's right, I don't." The bifocals switch back to the *Times.*

"What I'm saying is that what you really want to say is you want dick." The young man announces wearily to the ashen sky.

"Thanks, I already have one," the older man also speaks into the air as if addressing an invisible bird. But he does take his eyes off *The New York Times* in his hand without, however, lowering it.

"Wiseguy."

"Question the virtue of wisdom?"

"That's not the question. How much do you have on you?"

"Dick?"

"Yeah. That's my name. What's it going to be? Yes or no?"

"No comment."

"You mean you want it."

"I told you I have one already."

"What you've got is not a dick, but worn-out pisser. And it can't even piss any more."

"Good enough for me."

"That's sick. You mean you go down on yourself?"

"Very ingenious. You must be an off-off-Broadway producer."

"That's sick. You hang in the closet and jerk off over you face."

"Sounds like quite a feat, don't you think?"

"Sick, that's what I think.

"I didn't say how I used it."

"Used what? The closet?"

"No, my dick."

"You didn't?"

"No, I didn't."

Pause. The young man spreads his legs a little wider before he speaks again.

"Okay, wiseguy, just give me twenty."

"Twenty what?"

"What? Twenty kisses on my ass . . . Come to think of it, that'll be extra."

Without looking at the young man the older gent looks around to see if there were any witnesses to the statement. No one in earshot.

"Twenty bucks? What for?"

"My time. You've taken up twenty dollars worth of my time already."

"And you fifty of mine."

"Wiseguy again. Dick or no dick, you've got to pay."

"This is a public bench."

"Not talking about the bench but my time."

"You seem to have plenty to spare."

"That doesn't give you the right to abuse it."

"What? The bench?"

"Enough of this. I have no time for people who're just looking."

"What? Looking at the lawn? The pigeons?"

"Just move on, you jerk."

"That a threat?"

"Go and jerk off somewhere else. But first the twenty."

"You're mugging me."

"I never use force. Hardly ever. Instead I call the cops."

"Who? What are you going to tell them? I stole from you?"

"Worse. You offered twenty for a feel. To a normal young man on his way to work, you creep."

"This bench is big enough for the two of us."

"Go tell someone else on another bench. In the meantime I may be losing business. People might think you're on."

"I sit where I please."

"You want me to make a scene? That'll cost you a couple hundred . . . I can follow you home and go up to your apartment, make a scene with your doormen."

"And how much for my dick?"

"Don't get sick on me. Just give me the twenty and we're buddies. You can even put your hand on my basket. Just for a few seconds, no more."

"Rotten fruit in that basket."

"And you're dying for it . . ."

"Dying, dying, dead. No, I'll make it a gift basket."

"That'll cost you . . ."

"I'm talking about mine. I'll dress it up, put a bow on it and donate it to a saint who can give it away to the poor. My fruits and apples and banana . . ."

"In other words, you enjoy being the Incredible Shrinking Man . . ."

Silence. It begins to drizzle. Suddenly the young man gets up, casually kicks the older gent in the ankle and walks away. The older gent reaches into his sock with a shaking hand, but then he manages to stand up and limp off, holding *The New York Times* over his head against the rain. It's a big park, room for everyone, whatever direction one takes, wherever one waits for someone.

The bench is slowly filling up with shiny beads of rainwater. Hard to tell what passes between them. They beam at one another and after a while move closer and mingle.

WAR, SEX, MONEY

BY NINA ZIVANCEVIC

The New York headquarters of the global law firm occupied the fifty-sixth floor of a steel, glass and hardwood skyscraper on Water Street. It was certainly no place for a tiny sparrow that had somehow flown inside. The bird traveled from one office to another, swallowed by a maze of corridors, until it finally dropped to the floor, then fainted from exhaustion on my desk. The temp at the next desk kept urging me to get rid of it before the supervisor arrived.

"What should I do, just throw it out the window, watch it fall fifty-six floors, crash into the sidewalk, unconscious, and die?" I asked.

"Of course," he said, barely lifting his eyes from a merger report he had been proofreading for the last six hours without a break. "You're wasting pre-cious time. Take it off your coffee break. Here, I'll get your coffee myself to save you time. Just get rid of the bird."

He left, and returned less than two minutes later, with my freshly filled coffee cup in hand. When he looked up, he almost dropped it on the floor.

"Oh, no!" he said. "It's still here! The bird's still here and you haven't figured out how to get rid of it! Now we're headed for real trouble."

He sat the cup down and glanced at the stack of papers on my desk. His tone turned patronizing. "How much time did you spend on your document?"

"Thirty-four minutes and fifteen seconds," I teased.

"Impossible," he said. "You arrived here at 2 p.m., nearly six hours ago."

"So what?"

"Well . . . that means . . . that means . . . You can only stay here until midnight, you know. Until the third shift arrives, and then you're out . . ."

"Huh?"

"I'm telling you: You won't be able to make any money now, no money whatsoever, at this pace. Taking care of a bird—it's just ridiculous! By the way, my name is Roger. Are you an actress or something?"

He caught me off guard. I thought about it. In a way, I was an actress, like any immigrant new to New York City. I had struggled to attain success, one of the notions that seemed important to the American spirit. From what I could tell, success here came from a combination of three words: sex, war and money. Understanding the nuances of when and where to apply these was confusing, to say the least. An actress? Was Roger hitting on me? Starting a fight? Or trying to decide if I had any money?

"No, I am not an actress," I said.

"Well, you look like one . . . " he sighed. "I remember the last time I was in this law firm, a few months ago. I worked sixty-four hours straight—no sleep. This guy next to me just could not get into his work. He was an actor . . . Jim—yes, his name was Jim— that much I can recall, but I don't remember his face. He just sat there, where you're sitting now, and he ate sandwiches. He ate lots of sandwiches."

"Did he offer you any?" I asked.

"You must be kidding," Roger said. "Why should he? Would you offer your sandwiches to someone you've never seen before in your life?"

"Yes."

"You would," he snapped. "You'd try to save a bird too—because you are craaazy. Where do you come from? I mean, are there more people like you in your home country?"

"I'm from Nevada," I said flatly.

End of conversation.

A huge woman, head of the word processing department, slid like a galleon into our tiny office. Mary Lou weighed close to 300 pounds and dressed in pink, which made her look even heavier. She carried an enormous plastic tray filled with legal documents.

"Good evening, Mary Lou! How are you today?" Roger seemed delighted, as if this ample lady were Our Lady of Salvation herself.

Mary Lou acknowledged him by setting the tray down.

"Here are two very important agreements for the Brown Wood firm which have to be done right away," she announced with utmost urgency.

She glanced at the piles of unfinished work still on our desks.

"You two seem to be on the slow side tonight," she observed.

"Well, Ma'am," Roger chirped, "I've been trying to do my best but my partner has brought in this bird . . ."

"Bird?" Mary Lou asked.

"This—what should we call it?—this sparrow." Roger pointed. "There, on the second debenture. Yes, Leah— . . . Oh, what's your name again? Nina, right? Well, Nina brought the bird in and she kept parading around with this half-dead thing, wondering what to do with it. I told her to throw it out."

I had to defend the honor of the bird and myself.

"Excuse me," I explained. "The bird flew in through an A/C vent or a window or something and couldn't find its way out. I found it on the floor, in the corridor next to Mr. Holmes' office. I brought in here and it fainted on my desk."

"What does this have to do with legal documents?" Mary Lou asked sharply.

"It has to do with empathy, with respect for life!" I cried. I detected a dangerously high-pitched tone in my voice. "I can't simply let this little bird die! People kill so easily, without thinking twice. Soon, we'll become an endangered species, too!"

My ecological rap seemed to mellow Mary Lou. The expression on her face suddenly changed from annoyance to indifference. She glanced at the bird and let out a heavy sigh.

"Okay," she said. "Take the bird out and do whatever you wish with it."

I smiled. Roger snarled.

Mary Lou snapped, "But come back immediately, these debentures cannot wait!" She left abruptly, a thick curtain of dust trailing behind her.

I was already halfway through the door, carefully clutching my poor bird in the palms of my hands, when Roger squeaked like a parakeet, "Come back immediately, these debentures cannot wait!"

I wheeled around. "Don't repeat her words!" I shouted. "They sound even uglier coming from you!"

He acted like he didn't hear me.

This is war, I thought.

How did our conflict start? Did I unleash some inner demon in Roger that caused him to act so callously about the bird's existence? Did he clash with me because, deep down in his heart, he knew that I was right, that I had to defend this little creature against the corporate world?

In the claustrophobic elevator, I watched as the bird struggled for its life. This sparrow had nothing to do with the word processing department. It was there by chance. It didn't exist to earn money, wasn't there to start a war, and—at least in this environment—it had no mate.

I knew that once I released the sparrow on Water Street, it would not return.

Would I?

As soon as I passed the turnstile in the lobby, the bird lifted its head. Weak as it was, it nearly wiggled out of my hand and tried to fly away. I gently placed it on the sidewalk, next to a trashcan filled with soda cans and half-eaten hot dogs.

I stared as the bird struggled to its feet. It hopped a bit, and began nibbling at a discarded hot dog bun. It already seemed much better off than I ever was in the office, swimming in the word-processing pool on the fifty-sixth floor. Six hours of suffocating amidst the papers seemed like an eternity. Would I ever leave that pool? Could I do it now?

No. Not today. I stumbled back into the lobby and got in the elevator.

When I got back to the office, my tragic musings must have been visible on my face. Roger glanced up and snapped, "Back so soon? You know, for a second I thought that you'd left for good."

"I almost did."

"Yeah, but you know better," he said. "Guess you need the money. Now you can redouble your efforts and prove that you deserve the money you earn. Here, take this debenture. We have to scan it for errors by reading it together. I'll read out loud. Stop me if anything's wrong."

He handed me the papers and started to read. He read faster and faster, his curly head swirling around, hypnotized by legal language, his body shaking like a Dervish doing a strange corporate Sufi dance. I barely managed to keep up with him.

Suddenly, mid-sentence, he stopped and asked, "Would you like to have dinner with me tonight?"

I shuddered.

"I thought you wanted to stay here and work until dawn?"

"Well, that's true," Roger stammered. "But at the same time I started thinking that you had a nice body, uhmmmso . . . I thought we might have dinner instead."

I wasn't sure what "dinner" had to do with my body. Someone once informed me that in America, dinner was always followed by sex and no one could change the rules.

I was hungry, but . . . Didn't he know we were at war?

"No," I said firmly.

Roger seemed shocked.

"Are you sure?" he asked.

"Absolutely."

"Why?"

"Well, it's like this," I said. "Roger—you and I are at war, but don't ask me why. If we were to sign a sudden truce, and I had dinner with you, we would eat, and then you would want to have sex. Then we'd be back in the office tomorrow to earn money and the war would start again. War. Sex. Money. For you and most of America, this may mean success, but for me, it is infinitely more important to save the life of a bird."

Roger didn't say another word.

When we clocked out, we left the building in separate elevators.

A CLOWN A DAY

BY ANGELA SLOAN

Pauline sat alone at a wooden table for two, drinking coffee from a china cup in the West Village café of the Jane Hotel. She swirled the contents with a French-manicured finger, glanced at her watch, and adjusted the sleeves of her cashmere cardigan.

The cafe wasn't crowded. Nearby, an older couple read their respective newspapers. Soft music played from overhead speakers.

The door swung open and an attractive woman limped in. Her designer handbag matched her shoes. The left one was missing a heel.

"Hey Tash—!" Pauline said, fingering a long lock of hair.

"Hey Paul—! I'm so sorry to be late. I broke my pump in a subway grate."

"Thought that only happened in the movies. You okay?"

Natasha sat down and removed her large dark sunglasses revealing a pair of eyes coated in smudged black mascara and faded eye shadow—remnants of the previous night.

"Yeah, yeah, I'm okay," Natasha said. "But the strangest thing just happened. I was rescued . . ."

"Rescued?"

"A man in a clown suit saved me."

"A clown suit?"

"Yeah!" Natasha said. "I was walking down Fourteenth Street, when my left Jimmy Choo wedged itself in a grate. I tried to wriggle free, but the heel broke and I started falling, face-first, toward the sidewalk. Then, suddenly, I was caught in the arms of this tall, tacky clown, who stood me back up—and handed me my shoe!"

"Sounds like some kind of fairy tale, Tash."

"It was more like a drug-induced dream." Natasha said. "We looked into each other's eyes, then I took the shoe from the clown and stared like an idiot with my mouth gaping open as he walked off down

Fourteenth Street! I shouted 'thank you,' but I don't think he heard."

"That's incredible. Did you say he also sprayed you with one of those goofy rubber daisies? Your mascara's smudged."

"No," Natasha said. "Michael slept over."

"I thought you dumped that sleaze-bag."

"I did, but last night he called me up crying that his wife kicked him out," Natasha said. "And he wanted me to make him a peanut butter and jelly sandwich."

A waitress hovered at the table. Natasha ordered coffee with skim milk and a chocolate croissant.

"Did you make it for him? The sandwich?"

"Hell, no. You know there's never any food in my apartment. Only saltines and ginger-ale for when I get an upset stomach."

"You're a slut, Tash." Pauline crossed her legs and flicked small pieces of lint from her cardigan and watched them float to the floor.

"Slut? Don't be such a prude, Paul. Since when have I had a squeaky-clean reputation to uphold, anyway?"

The waitress delivered the order. Natasha poured two pink packets of artificial sweetener into her coffee, and stirred it with a silver spoon. "What'd you do this weekend?" she asked.

"You know . . . caught up on some laundry," Pauline said. "Went grocery shopping and found these greats figs. They're just wonderful. Then I had a manicure, pedicure, and eyebrow wax, and later I went to lunch with Mom. Chinese. Then Bob came over and—. . . Can I have a bite of your croissant?"

"Wait a minute. Bob? The dental hygienist? What'd he do, floss your teeth?"

Pauline sipped her coffee, adjusted her glasses and twirled her hair. "Actually, he was dressed as a clown." She took a large bite of the croissant.

"What? Where are all of these goddamn clowns coming from? Are they in the water supply? The clown who saved me was definitely not Bob. He was much, *much* taller, and not as swarthy."

"You sound like a bigot, Tash."

"I only speak honestly. That's why you love me."

"Never mind that," Pauline said. Lowering her voice, she added, "Bob wanted to do it in the clown suit."

"What?!" Natasha said.

"At first I didn't want to do it. I thought it would be strange—demented even—like those Cindy Sherman photographs."

"It is strange," Natasha said. "So what happened? I want details. Juicy ones. Don't leave anything out."

"We kissed for a while, and I got undressed. We started to fool around; all I remember after that is falling over. I fainted! I was out cold for like five minutes. He had to honk his toy horn in my ear to wake me up."

Natasha spat out a mouthful of coffee and howled with laughter. The other people in the cafe stared. She covered her mouth and took a bite of the chocolate croissant, and whispered, "What do you mean you fainted? From shock? Fear? What?"

"Not exactly . . ."

"You wild bitch!"

"Stop making fun! I knew I shouldn't have told you. You'll probably tell my mother for Christ's sake."

"It was that good, huh?" Natasha asked. "Lucky girl. It's about time! So, was Mr. Right wearing those dumbass floppy shoes?"

"He was wearing orange ones, if you must know. And a polka-dot bowtie. But I think it was the big red nose that did it."

"How did you kiss if he had that nose on? Did he wear a wig too?"

"It was purple and sparkly, and we kissed just fine." Pauline said. "I had to shower twice with Lava soap to get all his greasepaint makeup off me! There were red lip prints on the bottoms of my feet, and glitter under my toenails! I had to use the rough side of a kitchen sponge, you know, the wiry side, to get clean. My skin is practically raw."

"I bet there are some other raw places too," Natasha said.

The women doubled over with laughter.

"Who would've guessed?" Natasha asked. "All these years of reading *Cosmopolitan* and going to all of those horrible body awareness classes and all it takes to make your eyes roll back in your head is a dentist in a clown suit."

"He's actually a very gifted dental hygienist—the best man I know with a tongue scraper. You want his number?"

"Only if he brings a tank of laughing gas." Natasha licked her lips. "What did he use the tongue scraper for?"

"I'll tell you when you're thirty-five. And trust me honey; you won't need any laughing gas. You might need some new soap; I suggest something with pumice."

They burst out laughing again.

After they calmed down, Natasha asked, "What about that vibrating bug I gave you as a birthday present last year? Should I buy one too, or what?"

Pauline hugged herself. "What do you mean?"

"What do you think I mean? Come on. Was it as good as the magic clown?" Natasha licked the chocolate from her fingers and brushed the crumbs to the floor.

"I have a confession to make, Tash," Pauline said. "I never used that thing. It gives me the creeps. It's just too weird."

"You're one to talk about weird sex, Pauline. Don't think I've forgotten the homeless magician or the tattooed guy from Coney Island. And now this clown guy? Besides, that thing cost me nearly a hundred dollars."

Pauline looked down and twisted her hair. "I'm afraid of insects," she said.

"It wasn't real!" Natasha laughed. "It was only plastic, Paul. You're a nut!"

"I liked the tattooed guy," Pauline said. She placed a twenty on the table. "Let's just get out of here. I'll pay you back for the stupid caterpillar vibrator if that's what you want."

The women drained their coffee, grabbed their purses in hand and stood. Natasha suddenly stared across the room. "Hey, isn't that an Olsen twin over there? You should give her Bob's number. She looks pretty tense."

"Don't do that! Someone might see." Pauline covered her mouth to stifle her laughter.

Outside, they stared as an attractive young woman dressed in a Diane Von Fürstenberg wrap dress exited a taxi, followed by a man dressed as a clown, complete with a glittery wig, over-sized bowtie and big floppy shoes. Before parting ways, the clown and the woman shared a passionate, open-mouthed kiss.

"What the hell is going on in this city?" Natasha said. "Where did all of these fucking crazy clowns come from?"

"Haven't got a clue," Pauline said. "But thank God they're here."

They started to giggle and walked down Jane Street, arms entwined.

THE *REAL* NORTH EIGHTH STREET ROMANCE

BY RICHARD VETERE

He thought his *real* North Eighth Street romance was with Georgia. That summer he was the only guy who was either brave enough or stupid enough to ask her out. She had just broken her engagement with Gabe in June, and every night that summer when he went to the Miami Bar on North Eighth Street she'd be there hanging out with girlfriends. And like clockwork, early in the night, she'd leave the table and saunter across the room to play "Jumpin' Jack Flash" on the jukebox.

Though new to hanging out on North Eighth Street, he knew this much: Gabe managed a well-known rhythm and blues band and his father was a wise-guy, but Georgia was knock-out sexy.

He asked his cousin Little Guy if he should ask her out since Little Guy knew the world of Williamsburg, Brooklyn and its rules better than he did. "Shit yeah," Little Guy answered. So he made a plan. He'd walk up to the jukebox where nobody could hear them talk, ask her out and then leave the bar. His friend Frankie would already be in the car and they'd drive away. It was like a hit, but one for romance.

So, the next night he sat at the bar with one eye on Gabe and the other on Georgia. She was on the other side at the table and just like he expected she walked over to the jukebox and played "Jumpin' Jack Flash." He slid up beside her at the jukebox. "Georgia, you want to go out?" was all he said.

"Alright," she answered, surprised. She then told him her number and like he planned he left the bar.

He took Georgia to a wine cellar for their first date. "Nobody in the neighborhood had the guts to ask me out but you," she said. She had soft brown eyes, shoulder length hair, a slender build, a confidence that enticed him and the hottest ass he had ever seen. He asked her more about her relationship with Gabe. "We've been engaged twice now. But this time, I realized he wasn't the right guy for me. So I ended it."

He took her back to his parents' house in Queens where he lived in the finished basement and they had sex for the first time. They continued to have sex for the next two weeks and never did much talking. The sex play came easy to them both. He liked how she taught him new things and he taught her.

The only thing that concerned him was getting her pregnant. She didn't like it when he pulled out. He remembered how his Uncle Sal always talked about how his life was changed for the worse when he got his first wife pregnant. So despite being enthralled by Georgia, he was also suspicious.

One night in the Miami Bar a guy he hardly knew came up to him and told him that Gabe wanted to see him. His cousin Little Guy told him not to go but he went to the Miami Bar alone anyway. Gabe was waiting for him. "You got balls. I like that," Gabe said then pinched his cheeks.

Later that night Georgia told him "You shouldn't have given him the respect." She then invited him to a close friend's wedding the following weekend.

That night when they had sex she took off her panties and said, "These are my girlfriend Mary Jane's." They were red and see-through. "You'll meet her at the wedding. You're going to fall in love with her. Every man who meets her *does*."

He and Georgia arrived at the wedding late and when they walked in he saw a woman wearing a black dress dancing slowly with a man in a suit in the middle of the dance floor. The woman was crying. He was mesmerized by the sight of this beautiful dark-haired woman with tears rolling down her face dancing as she did. "That's Mary Jane," Georgia told him.

Minutes later Mary Jane was sitting next to him. The guy went off to another table. He handed Mary Jane a handkerchief. "Thank you," she said. Up close she was even more than beautiful. She was a light skinned Sicilian-American with lush brunette hair and deep green eyes. They made small talk but she eventually told him that she was crying because she broke up with the man she was dancing with. "He wouldn't leave his wife for me," she said.

When the wedding was over he got her jacket. "You keep doing nice things for me, "she said. "Georgia said you're a good guy."

"Georgia said I'd fall in love with you," he told her.

Two weeks later he ran into her and asked her out under the false pretense that Georgia left him and he needed to talk about it. A week later he was in bed with her in her apartment on Manhattan Avenue. He recognized her red see-through panties.

Mary Jane saw that he did. "I gave them to Georgia to wear one night," she demurred. "She told me she wore them with you."

He told his cousin Little Guy he was seeing Mary Jane. "You're crazy. You were better dating a mob guy's ex than that broad. Grown men go nuts over her. I knew this made-guy that when she broke up with him last year he shot up a bar on Knickerbocker Avenue he was so distraught. Watch yourself."

He should have listened to his cousin but he had no control because like other men before him he was beguiled by her perfect breasts, her perfect ass, the perfect face and how uninhibited she was in bed. Mary Jane was also the most sensitive woman he had ever met. She cried often and without reason. Both her parents were beautiful and born deaf. Her father was a national weight lifting champion. When she was only nineteen, she married a big deal mob guy's son who three months into their marriage walked out to buy a pack a cigarettes and never came back. He died less than a year later in a head-on car crash with a drunk driver on the LIE.

His father made the other driver, a junkie, 'disappear' the day of his son's funeral. Mary Jane never divorced him and the father took care of her for a few years by sending her cash.

He took Mary Jane everywhere including his college graduation dance. She made the college girls look like high school kids and his friends were enthralled by the fact that she was a gorgeous widow. But his mother never liked her and Mary Jane knew it. Mary Jane demanded attention and when she didn't get it, she made the world suffer. One day it was his turn. She moved to Queens and he helped her get settled in. She had a small hole in door where her old lock was so he promised he'd fill it.

Not long after, the day he found out that he was accepted into an Ivy League graduate school and they went out to celebrate, when they got back to her place, she broke up with him. "You're too immature for me," she said. It broke his heart.

For several months he defied common sense and begged her to take him back. He called all his friends day and night talking about nothing else.

One night, after calling her number all day, he went to her new apartment uninvited. She didn't answer his knocks on the door so he leaned down and peeked in through the hole where the old lock was that he never got the chance to fix.

He saw her sitting nude in a chair on the other side of the room facing the door in the dim light of a lit candle. He could see her green eyes gleaming and her full, dark hair cascading down over her shoulders. She was staring at the peep hole. Her flesh was more tempting than the promise of a long healthy life is to the dying. She was everything mysterious, alluring, sexual and dangerous.

He turned away and never went back.

DANGEROUS GIRL

BY LIZ AXELROD

I met Cosmo and Dante at the Aztec Lounge on the last Friday of 1986. Cosmo was a spoken-word artist with an album on the college charts. Dante was a dealer posing as a record label exec. They flattered me with poetry and followed me around the bar all evening—ready with a drink, a line, or a joint at every turn. I knew they wanted to get into my miniskirt but I kept them at bay, relishing the ego boost.

I supplied Goth themed mix-tapes to the manager of Aztec and occasionally slept with Michael, the bartender. Aztec was my usual starting and ending point, though most nights I went home alone. I sported East Village DJ couture. My nightly ensemble: ripped black fishnets, black leather jacket, black miniskirt, tons of silver bangles, and black cowboy boots from Tucson, AZ. Cosmo resembled a young deranged Einstein in his white poet shirt and tight black jeans, Dante wore a black Lurex disco shirt and Jordache jeans. I loved the contrast between us, and Dante's never-ending supply of white powder made it all the more interesting.

We enjoyed our playtime at Aztec and then grabbed a cab to the Voodoo Lounge where I worked as a DJ from 10 to 1, warming up the too-early-for-after-hours crowd. Cosmo carried my crate of records. I got him in the club for free (saving him 15 bucks) and headed to the DJ booth.

My music that night was red-hot. I segued Siouxsie and the Banshees with NWA, mixed Madonna and The Belle Stars with Beastie Boys, and looped The Cure's "Let's Go to Bed" with Michael Jackson's "Beat It." Guys crowded my booth, asking me to play their songs, and used rolled-up twenty-dollar bills to snort lines off my album covers. I was in my zone that evening at Voodoo. With New Year's Eve just around the corner, holiday spirits and tips were plentiful.

I partied with the rainbow. Nothing was ever black and white, the whole Pantone Process ran through my blood. I flirted and danced with boys and girls, all walks and tracks allowed. I spoke conversational Spanish and French, mixed Hip-Hop and Soul with Alternative Dance, and hung out with homeboys, mohawk men, goth girls, and Euro trash—sometimes all in the same evening. The club scene was hot downtown and I'd cultivated relationships with the doormen at the Milk Bar, Mudd Club, Danceteria, Mars, and Area. When I went out, I never waited in line. I was whisked right past the velvet rope and led to the VIP room.

Maybe I was naïve, maybe lucky, maybe just more tuned into my surroundings. I looked into the eyes of my playmates and knew who was safe and who to walk away from; skin tone optional. I prided myself on my powers of persuasion and rarely encountered problems. Potential conflict was usually diffused with a line of coke, a joint, or a slow dance.

II

Cosmo came back to the DJ booth a few minutes after midnight flirting and teasing me with his words.

"Hey Tina Turntable, I wrote you a poem. When you're finished spinning come find us. We wanna take you uptown to a great new club."

"Hmmm, uptown? Well, maybe, we'll see . . . You know, I'm not much of an Uptown Girl.

"You'll love it, don't worry. Let's meet up when you're done spinning. Damn, I just love your DJ name . . . Tina Turntable is so much fun to roll around your tongue." He winked and patted my ass.

"Roll this." I flipped him off—somewhat friendly like. "I gotta go play "Pretty in Pink" for some prep dude's Barbie doll blondie, he gave me a twenty."

He smiled and walked away, whispering something to Dante. They both looked my way and laughed.

I got paid for my shift and bought some more party goods. I found Cosmo sitting in the back of the VIP room with Dante, Steve—the Voodoo doorman—and Tommy from the Milk Bar. I was psyched to see Tommy in their company. I knew him casually from the Milk Bar. He had a quiet-tough vibe and I found his rough blond biker groove extremely compelling.

I sat down next to him and ignored Cosmo and Dante. Tommy smelled like earth and sex. His moves were catlike and sinewy. His stare conveyed tangible heat. When he flashed a smile my way and focused his deep blue eyes on mine, I was ready to burn.

Tommy was the main reason I threw caution to the wind when Cosmo and Dante said we should all go up to the new club in Harlem. I didn't think anything of heading uptown in Steve's boat-sized Marquis. I was just pleased to sit next to Tommy in the back seat. I shared my coke with them and we passed around a couple of joints. I made Steve play one of my mix-tapes. I could tell my Gothic dance mix really wasn't his style, but I downplayed the groans of displeasure.

"Get over it guys, it's good shit, plus there's Hip Hop coming up soon, I put some Beastie Boys and Prince on this tape."

"It's a damn good thing you're cute, girlie, cause your music sucks." Dante laughed and I shrugged it off.

Tommy gave me a raised eyebrow and I shrugged that off.

At the club we were ushered into a quiet VIP area. We crowded into a booth in the back of a dark, wood-paneled lounge with a professional billiards table. The seats were blood-red leather and the bar was lined in 50's cherry Formica. I drank Grand Marnier and made jokes. I danced around the table while Cosmo read a poem he wrote for me:

> *She breathes the mystery winds*
> *And dances on the ceiling.*
> *She's a dangerous lady spinning*
> *black vinyl in the void.*

Flattered, I laughed and told him it sounded a little like The Cars' "Dangerous Girl." I guess he didn't like the comparison, even though in my mind it was a compliment. He left the table and went over to shoot pool with Dante and Steve.

I sat down next to Tommy. He looked way out of place with his spikes and leather in a club filled with Member's Only jackets and velvet track suits, but he grabbed my hand and smiled. We talked quietly for a while and ignored the rest of the club. We laughed at the black light posters of *Superfly* and *The A Team* and enjoyed a bit of fun, flirty conversation. When he got up to make a phone call I joined Dante and Cosmo to do a few more lines and shoot some pool.

I scratched on the eight ball, much to my friend's chagrin, and headed to the bathroom. Dante and Cosmo followed.

After freshening my lipstick and wiping the powder off my nose, I found them both outside the bathroom door. They asked if I wanted to do another hit and motioned me to the stairway door.

"Sure, I'm up for it." We went into the stairway. Cosmo put the powder on his hand and I snorted it from the web between his thumb and finger.

"Thanks." As I turned to go back Dante put his hand on my waist and spun me around.

"You know . . . we been giving you blow all night. I think it's time you give something in return."

"Sure, man. No problem. I have some coke too. Here. I got the next line." I reached into my purse. When I looked up Dante was eyeing my chest with an evil grin and Cosmo was shuffling back and forth, a line of spittle pooled in the corner of his mouth.

I wasn't thinking straight. I blurted out "What's up guys? Is there a problem?"

Dante stood tall and his tone changed from friendly to menacing.

"Yeah, DJ, my problem is . . . you out of your place up here. You been acting like hot shit and above it all night long. We brought you up here and all you been doing is sliding up next to that biker guy. You need to start sliding up to the ones that brung you. So . . . baby . . . this is what we want." He smiled and bared his yellow teeth. "Take that skirt off and show us your cunt."

Cosmo laughed. "Yeah Tina, let's go baby. Dangerous girl, show us what you got"

Before I could react Cosmo reached out and grabbed the hem of my skirt. His hand grazed my thigh and ripped into my stocking. I pulled back and slammed my silver bangles into his shoulder.

"What the fuck? You want what?!" Shocked, I screamed "MY CUNT! Who the hell do you think you are! How FUCKING dare you!"

Cosmo smacked my face and pushed me into the wall. I felt the blood rushing to my head. I tried to get loose and he grabbed my arm and pulled me closer into him. We were face to face and his breath was horrifying. His poetry was shit and I was a fool to have ever come uptown with him. Damn them both to hell. If I had been packing a weapon those bastards would no longer be on the planet.

I looked Cosmo dead square in his bloodshot black eyes.

Maybe he felt my intent because he paused and looked confused for a second.

Using that moment of confusion to wiggle free, I ran back to the club. The room was empty except for a couple of seedy guys at the pool table arguing over a missed shot.

Dante and Cosmo sauntered in right after me, looking like nothing happened. They sat down at a table with Steve and began whispering and gesturing.

Disheveled and stinging, my face flaming with pain and outrage, I put my hand to my cheek. This hot new club was just a Harlem bar full of druggies at 5:30am, and I was the only female in the room.

Coke made me talkative, active, funny, and friendly. But it sure wasn't having the same effect on my friends.

My paranoia rose to the surface, I watched their evil whispers and pictured the scene from *Accused* where Jodie Foster was raped by four guys on a pinball machine and everyone else in the room applauded.

Tommy stood alone by the bar. I made my way over to him.

He put his arm around me and whispered, "I think it's time for us to leave now, yes?"

Dante yelled, "You two best get on home now. Your girl's up way past her bed time."

I leaned into Tommy as he directed me to the door and out onto the sunlit avenue filled with bodegas and beauty shops.

I pulled my Ray Bans out of my purse and put them on with shaking hands, jarred into the early Harlem morning by the grinding of steel gates opening for business.

MISSING DAUGHTER

BY CHERA THOMPSON

My daughter's flight back to college was at seven tomorrow morning. She had to be at JFK by six, which meant she had to leave my sister's New York City apartment by five-thirty. She was twenty, lived at school and had negotiated her way around Europe by train. Still, I worried about her standing alone in the middle of a New York City block to hail a cab before dawn, then ride by herself to JFK. I had to go with her. I set my alarm.

"Mom, you don't have to!"

"It's no problem, really."

"It's crazy," my sister said. "A round trip cab will cost you a fortune."

"Really?"

"Look—just let her take my car service," my sister said. "They're good."

"Car service?"

"I use them all the time."

"You sure?" I asked. *Because this is my only daughter I'm entrusting them with.*

"Never had a problem."

"Well . . . I don't know . . . " *Does she know the drivers personally? How do they screen them?*

"C'mon Mom! I'm not a baby!"

"They're very reliable," my sister insisted. "Best in New York."

"For God's sake, I'm twenty years old," my daughter whined. "I was taking cabs all over Italy two years ago."

"With your friends, not by yourself," I pointed out, defending my paranoia.

"The doorman is down in the lobby twenty-four seven," my sister said. "He'll look out for her."

"Well . . . "

Maybe taking a cab round trip to JFK was a little over the top. My mind flashed back to my daughter's first day of school when I followed the school bus in my car. No seat belts! My husband called me a helicopter parent . . . always hovering.

I relented.

"Okay," I said. "Car service."

The alarm went off at four-thirty. I heard my daughter get up, then dozed off until she kissed me on the cheek. "Time to go," she said. "I'll wait for them downstairs."

"No, no—I'll go with you."

"Mom, you don't have to."

I hesitated. "You sure?"

My sister yelled from her bed. "For God's sake! The doorman's down there!"

And in that split second, something inside me gave in. Right there: In my nightgown, on the eleventh floor, at 5:15 a.m. In that split second I let go. Let go of being an overprotective, middle-aged mother from Ohio. In that split second I became a New Yorker.

"Call me when you get to the airport."

"My cell phone's dead. Forgot to charge the battery."

"Well, find a pay phone."

"Okay, okay." She grabbed her suitcase, the door clicked shut and I sank back under the covers.

Fifteen minutes later, the intercom buzzed. What did she forget? I got up, still groggy, found my way to the button. "What is it, hon?"

"Car service."

"She's down there," I replied in a thanks-for-making-me-get-up, forced-hospitable sing-song.

"No one down here."

"No, she's waiting for you in the lobby. The redhead, the redheaded girl!"

"Nobody here."

"The doorman," I yelled. "Ask the doorman!"

"I don't see no doorman."

"Oh my God!" I screamed.

My sister shuffled into the room and turned on the light.

"No, no, no!" I shrieked, fumbling with the three locks on the door. I yanked it open and ran barefoot, in my nightgown, down the hall to the elevator.

My heart felt like a jackhammer. I pounded the button, wailing. I waited an eternity for the elevator to arrive and it took an eternity to go down eleven flights—ten and nine and eight and seven and— . . .

The elevator doors opened. The driver stood alone next to an empty front desk.

"Oh God, oh God! Where is she?" I whirled around the room. "Where the hell is the doorman?"

As if on cue, the doorman sauntered through the side door carrying an empty garbage can.

"Did you see my daughter?" I screeched.

"No," he said. He put the can by the door.

I grabbed his arm. "The redheaded girl with the suitcase?"

He sighed. "No one's been here."

"How do you know?" I squeezed his arm tighter. "Where were you?"

He yanked his arm away. "I took out the garbage. I was only gone five minutes."

"No! No!" I shook my head.

These are the five this-is-how-it-always-happens minutes. The I just went out to . . . break in routine that allows the kidnapping, the rape, the murder. The five missing minutes in the air-tight alibi, the detective crime novel, the never-again wonderful life.

I turned and ran out into the street, screaming my daughter's name. Garbage cans and mounds of plastic bags lined the curb. My beautiful girl could be among them, her tortured, twisted and mangled body stuffed into a plastic bag. Waiting for me to identify the slender fingers that loved to draw, the green eyes so calm and assured, the fair Irish skin.

I staggered back inside crying and pounded my fists against the glass door of the building. "Oh, this goddamned city!" I moaned, pounding, wanting to break the glass. Wanting the shards to stab my veins so I could bleed to death and the doorman could drag me out to the curb with the rest of the garbage. Me, the lazy mother who wouldn't ride down ten flights in an elevator and wait with my daughter for fifteen minutes even though I had guided her every move for twenty years.

My sister, the doorman and the driver tried to calm me down. They made phone calls to sort things out. I fell in a heap, banging my head on the floor, wanting to knock myself unconscious, or better, crack my head open so I could bleed out this nightmare and they could mop it up with my nightgown, then lug me out to the curb.

Oh, New York: The city that never gave you a break. Never gave you a five minute time-out from its horrid, vile, beating, shredding, stabbing . . .

"Stop it!" My sister shook me with one hand, balancing her phone in the other "Stop! They found her. She's all right. She's on her way to JFK."

"Huh? What?"

"The car service sent two cars. I never heard of that happening before, but that's what happened. She took the car that got here first. The dispatcher called the driver and she's in it."

"Are you sure?" I asked, lifting my head, sniffing and wiping my eyes. "Make sure. Ask the driver if the girl has red hair."

"I did. It's her."

The world stopped spinning. Everything rewound and fell back in place.

I pulled myself off the floor. The doorman stared at me with pity in his eyes. Pity for my Walmart nightgown twisted around my feet, pity for my racing heart, my swirling mind.

"I'm so sorry. So sorry," I sobbed, hugging him.

My tears dampened the shoulder of his navy jacket.

"You see, I'm from Ohio! And, well . . . "

Ohio! Where kids run free across unfenced lawns, not road-rage traffic. Where they ride in mini vans that say baby on board, not subways splattered with pornographic gang graffiti. What could he possibly know of Ohio?

"Please forgive me." I looked him straight in the eye.

"I understand," he said. "I have two girls myself."

My cab pulls up to my sister's building. I haven't stepped foot in New York City for six years. I walk into the lobby and there he is: The same doorman! Thinner. Smaller. Older. He must have seen thousands of people since the last time we spoke.

"Hello," I say. "Remember me?"

He doesn't blink. "Missing daughter."

The city forgives all. It's in the doorman's eyes. We smile.

A MOMENT OF
WRONG THINKING

A Matthew Scudder Story

BY LAWRENCE BLOCK

Monica said, "What kind of a gun? A man shoots himself in his living room, surrounded by his nearest and dearest, and you want to know what kind of a gun he used?"

"I just wondered," I said.

Monica rolled her eyes. She's one of Elaine's oldest friends. They were in high school together, in Rego Park, and they never lost touch over the years. Elaine spent a lot of years as a call girl, and Monica, who was never in the life herself, seemed to have no difficulty accepting that. Elaine, for her part, had no judgment on Monica's predilection for dating married men.

She was with the current one that evening. The four of us had gone to a revival of *Allegro*, the Rogers and Hammerstein show that hadn't been a big hit the first time around. From there we went to Paris Green for a late supper. We talked about the show and speculated on reasons for its limited success. The songs were good, we agreed, and I was old enough to remember hearing "A Fellow Needs a Girl" on the radio. Elaine said she had a Lisa Kirk LP, and one of the cuts was "The Gentleman is a Dope." That number, she said, had stopped the show during its initial run, and launched Lisa Kirk.

Monica said she'd love to hear it sometime. Elaine said all she had to do was find the record and then find something to play it on. Monica said she still had a turntable for LPs.

Monica's guy didn't say anything, and I had the feeling he didn't know who Lisa Kirk was, or why he had to go through all this just to get laid. His name was Doug Halley—like the comet, he'd said—and he did something on Wall Street. Whatever it was, he did well enough at it to keep his second wife and their kids in a house in Pound Ridge, in Westchester County, while he was putting the kids from his first marriage through college. He had a boy at Bowdoin, we'd learned, and a girl who'd just started at Colgate.

We got as much conversational mileage as we could out of Lisa Kirk, and the drinks came—Perrier for me, cranberry juice for Elaine and Monica, and a Stolichnaya martini for Halley. He'd hesitated for a beat before ordering it—Monica would surely have told him I was a sober alcoholic, and even if she hadn't he'd have noted that he was the only one drinking—and I could almost hear him think it through and decide the hell with it. I was just as glad he'd ordered the drink. He looked as though he needed it, and when it came he drank deep.

It was about then that Monica mentioned the fellow who'd shot himself. It had happened the night before, too late to make the morning papers, and Monica had seen the coverage that afternoon on New York One. A man in Inwood, in the course of a social evening at his own home, with friends and family members present, had drawn a gun, ranted about his financial situation and everything that was wrong with the world, and then stuck the gun in his mouth and blew his brains out.

"What kind of a gun," Monica said again. "It's a guy thing, isn't it? There's not a woman in the world who would ask that question."

"A woman would ask what he was wearing," Halley said.

"No," Elaine said. "Who cares what he was wearing? A woman would ask what his wife was wearing."

"A look of horror would be my guess," Monica said. "Can you imagine? You're having a nice evening with friends and your husband shoots himself in front of everybody?"

"They didn't show it, did they?"

"They didn't interview her on camera, but they did talk with some man who was there and saw the whole thing."

Halley said that it would have been a bigger story if they'd had the wife on camera, and we started talking about the media and how intrusive they'd become. And we stayed with that until they brought us our food.

When we got home Elaine said, "The man who shot himself. When you asked if they showed it, you didn't mean an interview with the wife. You wanted to know if they showed him doing it."

"These days," I said, "somebody's almost always got a camcorder running. But I didn't really think anybody had the act on tape."

"Because it would have been a bigger story."

"That's right. The play a story gets depends on what they've got to show you. It would have been a little bigger than it was if they'd managed to interview the wife, but it would have been everybody's lead story all day long if they could have actually shown him doing it."

"Still, you asked."

"Idly," I said. "Making conversation."

"Yeah, right. And you want to know what kind of gun he used. Just being a guy, and talking guy talk. Because you liked Doug so much, and wanted to bond with him."

"Oh, I was crazy about him. Where does she find them?"

"I don't know," she said, "but I think she's got radar. If there's a jerk out there, and if he's married, she homes in on him. What did you care what kind of gun it was?"

"What I was wondering," I said, "was whether it was a revolver or an automatic."

She thought about it. "And if they showed him doing it, you could look at the film and know what kind of a gun it was."

"Anybody could."

"I couldn't," she said. "Anyway, what difference does it make?"

"Probably none."

"Oh?"

"It reminded me of a case we had," I said. "Ages ago."

"Back when you were a cop, and I was a cop's girlfriend."

I shook my head. "Only the first half. I was on the force, but you and I hadn't met yet. I was still wearing a uniform, and it would be a while before I got my gold shield. And we hadn't moved to Long Island yet, we were still living in Brooklyn."

"You and Anita and the boys."

"Was Andy even born yet? No, he couldn't have been, because she was pregnant with him when we bought the house in Syosset. We probably had Mike by then, but what difference does it make? It wasn't about them. It was about the poor sonofabitch in Park Slope who shot himself."

"And did he use a revolver or an automatic?"

"An automatic. He was a World War Two vet, and this was the gun he'd brought home with him. It must have been a forty-five."

"And he stuck it in his mouth and—"

"Put it to his temple. Putting it in your mouth, I think it was cops who made that popular."

"Popular?"

"You know what I mean. The expression caught on, 'eating your gun,' and you started seeing more civilian suicides who took that route." I fell silent, remembering. "I was partnered with Vince Mahaffey. I've told you about him."

"He smoked those little cigars."

"Guinea-stinkers, he called them. DeNobilis was the brand name, and they were these nasty little things that looked as though they'd passed through the digestive system of a cat. I don't think they could have smelled any worse if they had. Vince smoked them all day long, and he ate like a pig and drank like a fish."

"The perfect role model."

"Vince was all right," I said. "I learned a hell of a lot from Vince."

"Are you gonna tell me the story?"

"You want to hear it?"

She got comfortable on the couch. "Sure," she said. "I like it when you tell me stories."

It was a week night, I remembered, and the moon was full. It seemed to me it was in the spring, but I could have been wrong about that part.

Mahaffey and I were in a radio car. I was driving when the call came in, and he rang in and said we'd take this one. It was in the Slope. I don't remember the address, but wherever it was we weren't far from it, and I drove there and we went in.

Park Slope's a very desirable area now, but this was before the gentrification process got underway, and the Slope was still a working-class neighborhood, and predominantly Irish. The house we were directed to was one of a row of identical brownstone houses, four stories tall, two apartments to a floor. The vestibule was a half-flight up from street level, and a man was standing in the doorway, waiting for us.

"You want the Conways," he said. "Two flights up and on your left."

"You're a neighbor?"

"Downstairs of them," he said. "It was me called it in. My wife's with her now, the poor woman. He was a bastard, that husband of hers."

"You didn't get along?"

"Why would you say that? He was a good neighbor."

"Then how did he get to be a bastard?"

"To do what he did," the man said darkly. "You want to kill yourself, Jesus, it's an unforgivable sin, but it's a man's own business, isn't it?" He shook his head. "But do it in private, for God's sake. Not with your wife looking on. As long as the poor woman lives, that's her last memory of her husband."

We climbed the stairs. The building was in good repair, but drab, and the stairwell smelled of cabbage and of mice. The cooking smells in tenements have changed over the years, with the ethnic makeup of their occupants. Cabbage was what you used to smell in Irish neighborhoods. I suppose it's still much in evidence in Greenpoint and Brighton Beach, where new arrivals from Poland and Russia reside. And I'm sure the smells are very different in the stairwells of buildings housing immigrants from Asia and Africa and Latin America, but I suspect the mouse smell is there too.

Halfway up the second flight of stairs, we met a woman on her way down. "Mary Frances!" she called upstairs. "It's the police!" She turned to us. "She's in the back," she said, "with her kids, the poor darlings. It's just at the top of the stairs, on your left. You can walk right in."

The door of the Conway apartment was ajar. Mahaffey knocked on it, then pushed it open when the knock went unanswered. We walked in and there he was, a middle-aged man in dark blue trousers and a white cotton tank-top undershirt. He'd nicked himself shaving that morning, but that was the least of his problems.

He was sprawled in an easy chair facing the television set. He'd fallen over on his left side, and there was a large hole in his right temple, the skin scorched around the entry wound. His right hand lay in his lap, the fingers still holding the gun he'd brought back from the war.

"Jesus," Mahaffey said.

There was a picture of Jesus on the wall over the fireplace, and, similarly framed, another of John F. Kennedy. Other photos and holy pictures reposed here and there in the room—on table tops, on walls, on top of the television set. I was looking at a small framed photo of a smiling young man in an army uniform and just beginning to realize it was a younger version of the dead man when his wife came into the room.

"I'm sorry," she said, "I never heard you come in. I was with the children. They're in a state, as you can imagine."

"You're Mrs. Conway?"

"Mrs. James Conway." She glanced at her late husband, but her eyes didn't stay on him for long. "He was talking and laughing," she said. "He was making jokes. And then he shot himself. Why would he do such a thing?"

"Had he been drinking, Mrs. Conway?"

"He'd had a drink or two," she said. "He liked his drink. But he wasn't drunk."

"Where'd the bottle go?"

She put her hands together. She was a small woman, with a pinched face and pale blue eyes, and she wore a cotton housedress with a floral pattern. "I put it away," she said. "I shouldn't have done that, should I?"

"Did you move anything else, ma'am?"

"Only the bottle," she said. "The bottle and the glass. I didn't want people saying he was drunk when he did it, because how would that be for the children?" Her face clouded. "Or is better thinking it was the drink that made him do it? I don't know which is worse. What do you men think?"

"I think we could all use a drink," he said. "Yourself not least of all, ma'am."

She crossed the room and got a bottle of Schenley's from a mahogany cabinet. She brought it, along with three small glasses of cut crystal. Mahaffey poured drinks for all three of us and held his to the light. She took a tentative sip of hers while Mahaffey and I drank ours down. It was an ordinary blended whiskey, an honest workingman's drink. Nothing fancy about it, but it did the job.

Mahaffey raised his glass again and looked at the bare-bulb ceiling fixture through it. "These are fine glasses," he said.

"Waterford," she said. "There were eight, they were my mother's, and these three are all that's left." She glanced at the dead man. "He had his from a jelly glass. We don't use the Waterford for every day."

"Well, I'd call this a special occasion," Mahaffey said. "Drink that yourself, will you? It's good for you."

She braced herself, drank the whiskey down, shuddered slightly, then drew a deep breath. "Thank you," she said. "It is good for me, I'd have to say. No, no more for me. But have another for yourselves."

I passed. Vince poured himself a short one. He went over her story with her, jotting down notes from time to time in his notebook. At one point she began to calculate how she'd manage without poor Jim. He'd been out of work lately, but he was in the building trades, and when he worked he made decent money. And there'd be something from the Veterans Administration, wouldn't there? And Social Security?

"I'm sure there'll be something," Vince told her. "And insurance? Did he have insurance?"

There was a policy, she said. Twenty-five thousand dollars, he'd taken it out when the first child was born, and she'd seen to it that the premium was paid each month. But he'd killed himself, and wouldn't that keep them from paying?

"That's what everybody thinks," he told her, "but it's rarely the case. There's generally a clause, no payment for suicide during the first six months, the first year, maybe even the first two years. To keep you from taking out the policy on Monday and doing away with yourself on Tuesday. But you've had this for more than two years, haven't you?"

She was nodding eagerly. "How old is Patrick? Almost nine, and it was taken out just around the time he was born."

"Then I'd say you're in the clear," he said. "And it's only fair, if you think about it. The company's been taking a man's premiums all these years, why should a moment of wrong thinking get them off the hook?"

"I had the same notion myself," she said, "but I thought there was no hope. I thought that was just the way it was."

"Well," he said, "it's not."

"What did you call it? A moment of wrong thinking? But isn't that all it takes to keep him out of heaven? It's the sin of despair, you know." She addressed this last to me, guessing that Mahaffey was more aware of the theology of it than I. "And is that fair?" she demanded, turning to Mahaffey again. "Better to cheat a widow out of the money than to cheat James Conway into hell."

"Maybe the Lord's able to take a longer view of things."

"That's not what the fathers say."

"If he wasn't in his right mind at the time. . ."

"His right mind!" She stepped back, pressed her hand to her breast. "Who in his right mind ever did such a thing?"

"Well. . ."

"He was joking," she said. "And he put the gun to his head, and even then I wasn't frightened, because he seemed his usual self and there was nothing frightening about it. Except I had the thought that the gun might go off by accident, and I said as much."

"What did he say to that?"

"That we'd all be better off if it did, himself included. And I said not to say such a thing, that it was horrid and sinful, and he said it was only the truth, and then he looked at me, he *looked* at me."

"What kind of a look?"

"Like, See what I'm doing? Like, Are you watching me, Mary Frances? And then he shot himself."

"Maybe it was an accident," I suggested.

"I saw his face. I saw his finger tighten on the trigger. It was as if he did it to spite me. But he wasn't angry at me. For the love of God, why would he. . ."

Mahaffey clapped me on the shoulder. "Take Mrs. Conway into the other room," he said. "Let her freshen up her face and drink a glass of water, and make sure the kids are all right." I looked at him, and he gave my shoulder a squeeze. "Something I want to check," he said.

I went into the kitchen, where Mrs. Conway wet a dishtowel and dabbed tentatively at her face, then filled a jelly glass with water and drank it down in a series of small sips. Then we went to check on the children, a boy of eight and a girl a couple of years younger. They were just sitting there, hands folded in their laps, as if someone had told them not to move.

Mrs. Conway fussed over them and assured them everything was going to be fine and told them to get ready for bed. We left them as we found them, sitting side by side, their hands still folded in their laps. I supposed they were in shock, and it seemed to me they had the right.

I brought the woman back to the living room, where Mahaffey was bent over the body of her husband. He straightened up as we entered the room. "Mrs. Conway," he said, "I have something important to tell you."

She waited to hear what it was.

"Your husband didn't kill himself," he announced.

Her eyes widened, and she looked at Mahaffey as if he'd gone suddenly mad. "But I saw him do it," she said.

He frowned, nodded. "Forgive me," he said. "I misspoke. What I meant to say was that the poor man did not commit suicide. He did kill himself, of course he killed himself—"

"I saw him do it."

"—and of course you did, and what a terrible thing for you, what a cruel thing. But it was not his intention, ma'am. It was an accident!"

"An accident."

"Yes."

"To put a gun to your head and pull the trigger. An accident?"

Mahaffey had a handkerchief in his hand. He turned his hand palm-up to show what he was holding with it. It was the cartridge clip from the pistol.

"An accident," Mahaffey said. "You said he was joking, and that's what it was, a joke that went bad. Do you know what this is?"

"Something to do with the gun?"

"It's the clip, ma'am. Or the magazine, they call it that as well. It holds the cartridges."

"The bullets?"

"The bullets, yes. And do you know where I found it?"

"In the gun?"

"That's where I would have expected to find it," he said, "and that's where I looked for it, but it wasn't there. And then I patted his pants pockets, and there it was." And, still using the handkerchief to hold it, he tucked the cartridge clip into the man's right-hand pocket.

"You don't understand," he told the woman. "How about you, Matt? You see what happened?"

"I think so."

"He was playing a joke on you, ma'am. He took the clip out of the gun and put it in his pocket. Then he was going to hold the unloaded gun to his head and give you a scare. He'd give the trigger a squeeze, and there'd be that instant before the hammer clicked on an empty chamber, that instant where you'd think he'd really shot himself, and he'd get to see your reaction."

"But he did shoot himself," she said.

"Because the gun still had a round in the chamber. Once you've chambered a round, removing the clip won't unload the gun. He forgot about the round in the chamber, he thought he had an unloaded weapon in his hand, and when he squeezed the trigger he didn't even have time to be surprised."

"Christ have mercy," she said.

"Amen to that," Mahaffey said. "It's a horrible thing, ma'am, but it's not suicide. Your husband never meant to kill himself. It's a tragedy, a terrible tragedy, but it was an accident." He drew a breath. "It might cost him a bit of time in purgatory, playing a joke like that, but he's spared hellfire, and that's something, isn't it? And now I'll want to use your phone, ma'am, and call this in."

"That's why you wanted to know if it was a revolver or an automatic," Elaine said. "One has a clip and one doesn't."

154

"An automatic has a clip. A revolver has a cylinder."

"If he'd had a revolver he could have played Russian roulette. That's when you spin the cylinder, isn't it?"

"So I understand."

"How does it work? All but one chamber is empty? Or all but one chamber has a bullet in it?"

"I guess it depends what kind of odds you like."

She thought about it, shrugged. "These poor people in Brooklyn," she said. "What made Mahaffey think of looking for the clip?"

"Something felt off about the whole thing," I said, "and he remembered a case of a man who'd shot a friend with what he was sure was an unloaded gun, because he'd removed the clip. That was the defense at trial, he told me, and it hadn't gotten the guy anywhere, but it stayed in Mahaffey's mind. And as soon as he took a close look at the gun he saw the clip was missing, so it was just a matter of finding it."

"In the dead man's pocket."

"Right."

"Thus saving James Conway from an eternity in hell," she said. "Except he'd be off the hook with or without Mahaffey, wouldn't he? I mean, wouldn't God know where to send him without having some cop hold up a cartridge clip?"

"Don't ask me, honey. I'm not even Catholic."

"Goyim is goyim," she said. "You're supposed to know these things. Never mind, I get the point. It may not make a difference to God or to Conway, but it makes a real difference to Mary Frances. She can bury her husband in holy ground and know he'll be waiting for her when she gets to heaven her own self."

"Right."

"It's a terrible story, isn't it? I mean, it's a good story as a story, but it's terrible, the idea of a man killing himself that way. And his wife and kids witnessing it, and having to live with it."

"Terrible," I agreed.

"But there's more to it. Isn't there?"

"More?"

"Come on," she said. "You left something out."

"You know me too well."

"Damn right I do."

"So what's the part I didn't get to?"

She thought about it. "Drinking a glass of water," she said.

"How's that?"

"He sent you both out of the room," she said, "*before* he looked to see if the clip was there or not.

So it was just Mahaffey, finding the clip all by himself."

"She was beside herself, and he figured it would do her good to splash a little water on her face. And we hadn't heard a peep out of those kids, and it made sense to have her check on them."

"And she had to have you along so she didn't get lost on the way to the bedroom."

I nodded. "It's convenient," I allowed, "making the discovery with no one around. He had plenty of time to pick up the gun, remove the clip, put the gun back in Conway's hand, and slip the clip into the man's pocket. That way he could do his good deed for the day, turning a suicide into an accidental death. It might not fool God, but it would be more than enough to fool the parish priest. Conway's body could be buried in holy ground, regardless of his soul's ultimate destination."

"And you think that's what he did?"

"It's certainly possible. But suppose you're Mahaffey, and you check the gun and the clip's still in it, and you do what we just said. Would you stand there with the clip in your hand waiting to tell the widow and your partner what you learned?"

"Why not?" she said, and then answered her own question. "No, of course not," she said. "If I'm going to make a discovery like that I'm going to do so in the presence of witnesses. What I do, I get the clip, I take it out, I slip it in his pocket, I put the gun back in his hand, and then I wait for the two of you to come back. And *then* I get a bright idea, and we examine the gun and find the clip missing, and one of us finds it in his pocket, where I know it is because that's where I stashed it a minute ago."

"A lot more convincing than his word on what he found when no one was around to see him find it."

"On the other hand," she said, "wouldn't he do that either way? Say I look at the gun and see the clip's missing. Why don't I wait until you come back before I even look for the clip?"

"Your curiosity's too great."

"So I can't wait a minute? But even so, suppose I look and I find the clip in his pocket. Why take it out?"

"To make sure it's what you think it is."

"And why not put it back?"

"Maybe it never occurs to you that anybody would doubt your word," I suggested. "Or maybe, wherever

Mahaffey found the clip, in the gun or in Conway's pocket where he said he found it, maybe he would have put it back if he'd had enough time. But we came back in, and there he was with the clip in his hand."

"In his handkerchief, you said. On account of fingerprints?"

"Sure. You don't want to disturb existing prints or leave prints of your own. Not that the lab would have spent any time on this one. They might nowadays, but back in the early sixties? A man shoots himself in front of witnesses?"

She was silent for a long moment. Then she said, "So what happened?"

"What happened?"

"Yeah, your best guess. What really happened?"

"No reason it couldn't have been just the way he reconstructed it. Accidental death. A dumb accident, but an accident all the same."

"But?"

"But Vince had a soft heart," I said. "Houseful of holy pictures like that, he's got to figure it's important to the woman that her husband's got a shot at heaven. If he could fix that up, he wouldn't care a lot about the objective reality of it all."

"And he wouldn't mind tampering with evidence?"

"He wouldn't lose sleep over it. God knows I never did."

"Anybody you ever framed," she said, "was guilty."

"Of something," I agreed. "You want my best guess, it's that there's no way of telling. As soon as the gimmick occurred to Vince, that the clip might be missing, the whole scenario was set. Either Conway had removed the clip and we were going to find it, or he hadn't and we were going to remove it for him, and *then* find it."

"'The Lady or the Tiger.' Except not really, because either way it comes out the same. It goes in the books as an accident, whether that's what it was or not."

"That's the idea."

"So it doesn't make any difference one way or the other."

"I suppose not," I said, "but I always hoped it was the way Mahaffey said it was."

"Because you wouldn't want to think ill of him? No, that's not it. You already said he was capable of tampering with evidence, and you wouldn't think ill of him for it, anyway. I give up. Why? Because you don't want Mr. Conway to be in hell?"

"I never met the man," I said, "and it would be presumptuous of me to care where he winds up. But I'd prefer it if the clip was in his pocket where Mahaffey said it was, because of what it would prove."

"That he hadn't meant to kill himself? I thought we just said. . ."

I shook my head. "That she didn't do it."

"Who? The wife?"

"Uh-huh."

"That she didn't do what? Kill him? You think <u>she</u> killed him?"

"It's possible."

"But he shot himself," she said. "In front of witnesses. Or did I miss something?"

"That's almost certainly what happened," I said, "but she was one of the witnesses, and the kids were the other witnesses, and who knows what they saw, or if they saw anything at all? Say he's on the couch, and they're all watching TV, and she takes his old war souvenir and puts one in his head, and she starts screaming. 'Ohmigod, look what your father has done! Oh, Jesus Mary and Joseph, Daddy has killed himself!' They were looking at the set, they didn't see dick, but they'll think they did by the time she stops carrying on."

"And they never said what they did or didn't see."

"They never said a word, because we didn't ask them anything. Look, I don't think she did it. The possibility didn't even occur to me until sometime later, and by then we'd closed the case, so what was the point? I never even mentioned the idea to Vince."

"And if you had?"

"He'd have said she wasn't the type for it, and he'd have been right. But you never know. If she didn't do it, he gave her peace of mind. If she did do it, she must have wondered how the cartridge clip migrated from the gun butt to her husband's pocket."

"She'd have realized Mahaffey put it there."

"Uh-huh. And she'd have had twenty-five thousand reasons to thank him for it."

"Huh?"

"The insurance," I said.

"But you said they'd have to pay anyway."

"Double indemnity," I said. "They'd have had to pay the face amount of the policy, but if it's an accident they'd have had to pay double. That's if there was a double-indemnity clause in the policy, and I have no way of knowing whether or not there was. But most policies sold around then, especially relatively small policies, had the clause. The companies liked to write them that way, and the policy holders usually went for them. A fraction more in premiums and twice the payoff? Why not go for it?"

We kicked it around a little. Then she asked about the current case, the one that had started the whole thing. I'd wondered about the gun, I explained, purely out of curiosity. If it was in fact an automatic, and if the clip was in fact in his pocket and not in the gun where you'd expect to find it, surely some cop would have determined as much by now, and it would all come out in the wash.

"That's some story," she said. "And it happened when, thirty-five years ago? And you never mentioned it before?"

"I never thought of it," I said, "not as a story worth telling. Because it's unresolved. There's no way to know what really happened."

"That's all right," she said. "It's still a good story."

The guy in Inwood, it turned out, had used a .38-calibre revolver, and he'd cleaned it and loaded it earlier that same day. No chance it was an accident.

And if I'd never told the story over the years, that's not to say it hadn't come occasionally to mind. Vince

Mahaffey and I never really talked about the incident, and I've sometimes wished we had. It would have been nice to know what really happened.

Assuming that's possible, and I'm not sure it is. He had, after all, sent me out of the room before doing whatever it was he did. That suggested he hadn't wanted me to know, so why should I think he'd be quick to tell me after the fact?

No way of knowing. And, as the years pass, I find I like it better that way. I couldn't tell you why, but I do.

ABOUT THE AUTHORS

LIZ AXELROD received her Masters of Fine Arts in Creative Writing at The New School in May of 2013. Her work has been published or is forthcoming in the *Cat Oars Fiction Collective, Lyre Lyre, 12th Street, The Rumpus, The Brooklyn Rail, Electric Literature, Yes Poetry, Nap Magazine* and the *Ginosko Literary Journal*.

LAWRENCE BLOCK has been chronicling the evolving life and times of Matthew Scudder for forty years and through seventeen novels and a dozen shorter works. LB s a devout New Yorker; when he's not walking the streets of Greenwich Village, you can find him hanging out at www.lawrenceblock.com

GIL FAGIANI is an independent scholar, translator, short story writer and poet. His most recent book of poetry is *Serfs of Psychiatry* (Finishing Line Press, 2012). He has translated poetry written in Italian and Abruzzese dialect into English. Gil co-curates the Italian American Writers' Association's monthly reading series in Manhattan, and is an Associate Editor of *Feile-Festa*.

BONNY FINBERG has been published in *The Brooklyn Rail, Evergreen Review, Ping Pong, Sensitive Skin, A Gathering of Tribes,* and the French literary journals *Upstairs at Duroc, Van Gogh's Ear* and *Le Purple Journal*. She has published two chapbooks: *How the Discovery of Sugar Produced the Romantic Era* and *Déjà Vu* and a novel, *Kali's Day*, published in 2014 by Autonomedia/Unbearable Books.

MICHAEL S. GATLIN has traveled across Canada in a carnival circuit, worked for the National Park Service clearing trails in Montana, and tried his hand at several other personalities. After twelve years of owning and operating Verlaine on the Lower East Side of Manhattan he has moved his family to Portland Maine.

KIRPAL GORDON is a born-&-bred NYC writer. For a free download of an excerpt from his latest eBook fiction project on music & mysticism, visit www.facebook.com/sullivanstpress. For a look at his blog on artists & activists, visit http://giantstepspress.blogspot. com. For more on the author, visit www.KirpalG.com.

RON KOLM is a member of the Unbearables and an editor of several of their anthologies, most recently *The Unbearables Big Book of Sex*. He is a contributing editor of *Sensitive Skin* and the editor of the *Evergreen Review* and is a fixture in the Lower East Side Literary Scene.

PETER MARRA, a Brooklyn native, is now 3-for-3 in the *HAVE A NYC* series. His chapbook *Sins of the Go-Go Girls* was published in April 2013 by Why Vandalism? Press. A short story, "Expert Collisions will appear in "From Somewhere to Nowhere: The End of the American Dream," due out in 2014 from Unbearable Books.

J. ANTHONY ROMAN is a playwright and fiction writer in New York City, where he was raised, after being a Puerto Rican volunteer refugee. Most of his plays have been produced in New York City, Los Angeles, and the UK. His fiction has been published by gadfly.com, *The Unboxed Voices Anthology*, and Rawboned.org. To follow his misadventures, please visit www.janthonyroman.com

ANGELA SLOAN currently co-edits a fashion-as-art column entitled "Closet Space" with her twin sister, Katherine, for *SPACES*, an online literary magazine. She earned her MA in English and Creative Writing from Longwood University in Virginia, and is currently living in New York City.

PAUL SOHAR ended his higher education with a BA in philosophy and took a day job in a research lab while writing in every genre, including seven volumes of translations and his own poetry: *Homing Poems* (Iniquity, 2006) and *The Wayward Orchard*, a Wordrunner Prize winner (2011). His other awards include first prize in the 2012 Lincoln Poets Society contest; second prize for a story from Writers' Circle of RI (2014).

CHERA THOMPSON is a teacher/writer living on a bluff over Lake Erie. Her story "Last Minute Pick-Up" received Honorable Mention in Glimmer Train's short fiction contest. Her work has appeared in *Roadside Fiction, Queen City Flash* and other publications. Her website is www.cherathompson.blogspot.com.

RICHARD VETERE is the author of three novels, including *The Writers Afterlife* (Three Rooms Press); *Baroque* (Bordighera Press) and *The Third Miracle* (Simon & Schuster); many plays, including *Caravaggio, Machiavelli, Gangster Apparel*; and movies, including *The Third Miracle, The Marriage Fool* and *Vigilante*. His short story "Champagne and Cocaine" (from HAVE A NYC 2) was nominated for a Pushcart Prize.

NINA ZIVANCEVIC is poet, essayist, fiction writer, playwright, art critic, translator and the Paris contributing editor to NY ARTS magazine. A former assistant and secretary to Allen Ginsberg, Nina has also edited and participated in numerous anthologies of contemporary world poetry.

JOANIE HIEGER FRITZ ZOSIKE makes as much mischief as is allowable in as many venues as possible. Onstage and off, she seeks the poetic grail and recycles whatever she can glean in publications including *Maintenant: A Journal of Contemporary Dada Writing and Art* (Three Rooms Press) and *NY Arts Magazine*. She is a member of The Living Theatre and director of DADAnewyork.

EDITORS

PETER CARLAFTES is an NYC playwright, poet, and performer. He is the author of twelve plays, including a noir treatment of Knut Hamsun's *Hunger*, and his own celebrity rehab center spoof, *Spin-Dry*. Carlaftes is the author of *A Year on Facebook* (humor), *Drunkyard Dog* and *I Fold With the Hand I Was Dealt* (poetry), and *Triumph for Rent* (3 plays). He is co-director and editor of Three Rooms Press.

KAT GEORGES is an NYC poet, playwright, performer and designer. She is the author twelve plays, including *SCUM: The Valerie Solanas Story* and *Art Was Here*, a creative look at Dada instigator Arthur Cravan. She is also author of the poetry collections *Our Lady of the Hunger* and *Punk Rock Journal* In New York since 2003, she has directed numerous Off-Broadway plays, curated poetry readings, and performed widely. She is co-director and art director of Three Rooms Press.